At first, Beth didn't recognize him...

He looked so different from the man she had once known.

Dizziness assailed her, but she struggled to her feet. The face she had known so well blurred before her. This couldn't be Clark, no longer a miner but a well-groomed executive, dressed in a dark suit, silk tie and white shirt, looking quite at ease in the intimidating corporate atmosphere.

But when he walked toward her, she knew it was true. Clothes couldn't change his graceful, easy tread or the steady, serene gaze that held her spellbound when he reached out his hand.

He smiled and greeted her. Needing desperately to steady her nerves, she gripped his hand. And felt overwhelmed by a rush of emotions.

Why had she ever come back? Beth wondered.

Books by Irene Brand

Love Inspired

Child of Her Heart #19
Heiress #37
To Love and Honor #49
A Groom To Come Home To #70

IRENE BRAND

This prolific and popular author of both contemporary and historical inspirational fiction is a native of West Virginia, where she has lived all of her life. She began writing professionally in 1977, after she completed her master's degree in history at Marshall University. Irene taught in secondary public schools for twenty-three years, but retired in 1989 to devote herself full-time to her writing.

In 1984, after she'd enjoyed a long career of publishing articles and devotional materials, her first novel was published by Thomas Nelson. Since that time, Irene has published nineteen contemporary and historical novels and three nonfiction titles with publishers such as Zondervan, Fleming Revell and Barbour Books.

Her extensive travels with her husband, Rod, to forty-nine of the United States and thirty-two foreign countries have inspired much of her writing. Through her writing, Irene believes she has been helpful to others and is grateful to the many readers who have written to say that her truly inspiring stories and compelling portrayals of characters of strong faith have made a positive impression on their lives. You can write to her at P.O. Box 2770, Southside, WV 25187.

A Groom To Come Home To

Irene Brand

Love Inspired®

Published by Steeple Hill Books™

STEEPLE HILL BOOKS

Steeple
Hill™

ISBN 0-373-87070-1

A GROOM TO COME HOME TO

Visit us at www.steeplehill.com

Printed in U.S.A.

To the following people who were helpful in my research for this book:

Beth Loughner, fellow writer and nurse
Gladys Hoskins, Chamber of Commerce,
Harlan, Kentucky
The staff at the public library in Harlan, and
Kathy Wheeler, who provided research material
about the Kentucky Coalition of Nurse Practitioners
and Nurse Midwives.

How priceless is your unfailing love!
—*Psalm* 36:7a

Chapter One

Long before she reached the top of Randolph Mountain, Beth Warner knew she had made a big mistake. Earlier in the day when she'd been heading westward toward Lexington, she should have resisted the impulse to visit southeastern Kentucky. She didn't cherish any fond memories of this part of the country where she had lived for eighteen years of her life. When she'd left over four years ago, she'd hoped she would never have to return, but there was no other way to repay the obligation she owed Shriver Mining Company.

The January day was clear and crisp, but it had snowed recently, and as she turned off the paved highway, Beth looked in dismay at the quagmire that passed for a gravel road leading up the side of the mountain. Deep ruts marked the slippery clay surface of the wet, narrow track. Could her small car possibly negotiate that incline? When she had traveled this road in other years, it had always been on foot or in her father's pickup truck.

Beth was afraid to tackle the hill, for she had owned the car less than a week, and she wasn't an experienced driver. Her driving expertise had already been tested to the breaking point on the narrow, serpentine road crossing Pine Mountain from Whitesburg to Cumberland, but at least there had been guardrails along that mountainous stretch. Here, one false move could send her over an embankment. But while she wasn't inclined to take any chances, she'd come too far to turn back now.

She started slowly, gripping the steering wheel with moist hands, and sat straight as a ramrod while she slowly and steadily maneuvered the compact automobile up the slippery road. She released her breath when she reached the summit. Her hands were clammy, and when she lifted her foot from the accelerator, her leg trembled.

She pulled to one side of the road and parked on the soft needles in a grove of hemlocks. The wind swept briskly across the mountaintop, whipping the branches of the tall evergreens and buffeting her car. Beth slipped off her shoes and pulled on a pair of wool-lined boots, wrapped herself in an insulated coat, and tied a wool scarf around her long, straight, chestnut hair before she looked for the path that would take her to the brink of the mountain. Briers, thick vines and small trees barred the path's entrance, but Beth walked around the underbrush and into the deeper woods where the trail was more distinct.

A ten-minute walk brought her to the edge of a

rock cliff, and from that vantage point, she had an unobstructed view of the rugged mountain hollow where she had been born.

"Just as ugly and wretched as I remember," she muttered.

Her eyes followed the crooked roadway leading into the small valley that showed no sign of life except for two crows perched in the leafless branches of a poplar tree, their harsh, strident cries echoing from one mountainside to the other. The towering cedars in the family cemetery where her parents were buried stood like watchmen over the hollow. A sparse snowfall had dusted the barren ground and the roofs of the deserted, ramshackle buildings, making the whole scene more desolate than it would have appeared in another season.

Even during the days when she had yearned to leave this hollow, Beth had always been sensitive to its beauty—the flowering redbud and dogwood trees in early spring, the green of the deciduous trees in the summer, and their yellow-and-red foliage in autumn. Today, however, she couldn't summon any nostalgic thoughts of the past; all she saw was ugliness.

Her birthplace hadn't changed a great deal from the way she first remembered it; in fact, Beth doubted that it had changed much since her ancestor had built a log cabin here soon after the Revolutionary War. During a rare period of prosperity, when Beth had been a toddler, her father had put siding over the logs and paneled the interior, but otherwise the four-room cabin with a full porch across the front seemed untouched by the years.

The scene was so deeply etched in Beth's memory that she wouldn't have been surprised to see her work-weary mother step out the door and draw water from the well in the backyard. Nor would it have seemed unusual to observe her invalid father, John, sitting in his favorite rocker on the front porch with a shotgun across his knees, his keen eyes searching the landscape for any unwelcome intruders in general, and Randolphs in particular. But except for the two crows, and Beth's poignant memories, the hollow was deserted. After John Warner's death, her half siblings had sold the property to a Shriver mining company, who wanted the land for the minerals lying beneath its surface.

A cold wind blew up from the hollow, indicating that more snow was a possibility. Beth shivered and headed back to her car. She had intended to go down to the house, but one glance at the road had discouraged her. The difficulty she'd had climbing Randolph Mountain was minor compared to the danger she would encounter on that narrow path. It would be foolish for her to attempt to drive into the hollow, for she couldn't risk being stranded overnight without shelter.

Beth had often heard, "You can't go home again," but she decided that a more accurate adage would be, "You shouldn't go home again." She'd yielded to a questionable whim to come here, but it had profited her little. Beth broke into a run as she left the overlook. Warner Hollow was too full of memories disturbing to her peace of mind, and she wanted to leave it as quickly as possible. She raced along the path, determined to escape the past—especially her heart-breaking relationship with Clark Randolph, who had rarely left her thoughts since that day she had first seen him over seven years ago.

As Beth left Randolph Mountain, recollections of the past persisted, and she concluded that she might as well deal with the bitterness she harbored and lay it aside forever. So, all during a sleepless night at a motel in Harlan, Kentucky, she reviewed the chain of events that had brought underprivileged Beth Warner from that stark mountain home and made her into Beth Warner, advanced registered nurse-practitioner and midwife, who tomorrow would be in the employ of Shriver Mining Company.

"Why do you want to go to high school, Beth? You'll be sixteen in a few months—you can quit school then. Why can't you be like the other girls around here?" Mary Warner asked in querulous tones. Mary was a quiet, submissive wife. Beth had inherited her petite, finely-structured body, but there the resemblance between mother and daughter ended.

"I don't know, Mom, but I can't. You know how I'm always feeling sorry for people who have trouble and wanting to help them. I want to prepare myself to help others, and I can't do it without more education than I have now."

"What's put all of this into your head? Some book you've been reading?"

"Maybe.... The teacher loaned me a book on the lives of great women in history, and I can't get the story of Florence Nightingale out of my mind," Beth confided. "She overcame all kinds of opposition to become a nurse and she helped so many people."

"Then you want to be a nurse?"

Dreamily Beth said, "Not necessarily, although it would be a profession where I could reach out and help others, and I can't do that if I don't go to school somewhere beyond these mountains."

"If you want to pattern your life after someone, why don't you use Granny Warner for a model?"

"I didn't know she was so important."

"Well, she was. You're always complaining about your poor family background, but let me tell you, there has never been a finer woman walked the earth than Granny Warner or my own mother, for that matter. And my father's people have served in every war this country has ever fought. As far as that's concerned, you've got a lot of good ancestors among the Warners. Why, the family has been in this country since the founding of Jamestown!"

"My brothers don't amount to much."

"Well, that's not Warner blood," Mary said and her mouth snapped shut, as if she would say no more, for she had always been jealous of John Warner's first wife.

"Tell me more about Granny Warner."

"She was the best midwife ever lived in Harlan County—she's the one who brought you into the world, as well as your sister and brothers. She traveled all over these mountains, any time of day or night, to help women give birth.''

"I'll never forget the time Luellen was here and Granny came and helped deliver her baby. But women go to hospitals for delivering their babies now.''

"Not all of them—some women still prefer to give birth at home.''

"But I believe that my destiny is some place other than Kentucky.''

Mary continued as if Beth hadn't spoken. "Granny Warner was trained by Mary Breckinridge, who recognized the need for midwives in the isolated areas of Kentucky, and she organized the Frontier Nursing Service back in the twenties. Your granny was proud to serve with her.''

"I could be a nurse and a midwife, too, I suppose, but it will still take more education than I have.''

Mrs. Warner sighed. "I wish you could be content with your life the way it is, but since you can't be, do what you think best. It won't be easy for you to go to high school. The bus line is over three miles away. You'll have to walk there and back most days, Beth.''

"I wondered if I could stay with Grandma Blaine during the week. The bus passes right by her house.''

"I'll ask her, but you'd better clear this with your daddy.''

Beth nodded, and she wandered out on the porch, mildly elated, for she didn't expect any resistance from her father, who had idolized his youngest daughter since the day Beth was born on his sixtieth birthday. John Warner was tall and lanky, a smooth-shaven man with bluish shadows beneath his dark eyes. John's health had never been good after having been a prisoner of war during World War II, and since his retirement from the mine, he had been disabled by heart disease. His portable oxygen tank lay on a table by his side, for John didn't dare go anyplace without it. Beth sat on the porch floor beside her father and took his hand.

"Why are you looking so serious, baby?" he asked.

"I want to go to school in the county seat this fall."

"You're such a smart girl—I figure you know everything now."

Beth shook her head stubbornly. "Not enough to get me away from this hollow."

A cloud passed over John's eyes. "Anxious to leave your old pa, are you?"

She squeezed the bony hand she held. "No, not that, Daddy, but don't you want me to have a better life than you've had?"

"Yes, I do, baby, even if it means you have to leave us. I can't keep you here forever. I reckon it will cost a heap of money to go to school in the county seat, but I'll give you all the help I can."

"Thanks, Daddy, but my teacher told me that there are funds available through your union to aid children of disabled miners. She's encouraged me to go on with school, and she'll help me fill out an application."

"You've got the makings of a great woman, Beth,

and if you think you need more schooling, go ahead and get it. I wish I'd had more book learning myself. After the war, I could have gone to school under the G.I. Bill, but I didn't. I've been sorry, too, that I didn't.'' He started talking about his war experiences, and Beth listened halfheartedly. She'd heard the stories so many times, but she looked at him intently, even while her thoughts turned to the future.

Fortified by her parents' agreement with her plans, Beth climbed the hill to her hideaway, a playhouse under a cliff that she'd used since she was a child. She always went there when she wanted to think, and she had a lot of thinking to do. She was sure that her maternal grandmother would welcome her, and if her father could contribute a little money, perhaps she could get the remainder she needed from the miners' union if her former teacher could advise her how to do it.

And the woman did recommend Beth for a grant, which was awarded immediately. More practical help came from a friend, Pam Gordon. Pam had married Ray Gordon when she was fifteen and moved to Pineville in a neighboring county. When Pam heard about Beth's plans, she insisted that Beth should pay her a visit.

''I'll help you find clothes that won't cost you a great deal,'' she promised. ''You won't need to buy new things. Since Ray is going to Lexington next week to play with his bluegrass band, we'll go along, and I'll take you to a 'second-best' store where they have really nice name-brand clothing for much less than you can buy it in retail stores. What you need are jeans and shirts, and if they're somewhat worn, it won't matter. High-school kids like them better that way." She laughed. Under Pam's guidance, Beth had come home from Pineville with enough outfits to satisfy her school needs.

Now, as she listened to a blustery wind blowing snow around the motel, Beth remembered how frightened she had been on the first day of school when she'd stood in front of Grandmother Ella Blaine's home and watched the yellow bus approaching.

For a moment, she wanted nothing more than to run back to the hollow and stay there for the rest of her life. She knew what awaited her at home, but if she stepped on the bus, an unknown future loomed ahead. *But should she give up her dreams so easily? Florence Nightingale hadn't.*

Fortunately, Beth's mind was diverted from her own problems when a couple of children, who lived in the house adjacent to her grandmother's, came out their door. The little boy was walking on crutches, his right leg encased in a cast. When they reached Beth's side, his sister explained, "Bryce broke his leg last week and since this is his first day at school, he's scared. Mom would have taken us this morning, but the baby is sick."

Beth looked at Bryce, whose lips were trembling, and his hands were shaking on the crutches.

"Come on, Bryce," she said. "There's nothing to be afraid of. I'll help you onto the bus."

When the bus stopped in front of them, the driver swung open the door and smiled at Beth. She threw the strap of her knapsack over her shoulder and held Bryce around the waist as he awkwardly climbed the steps. The bus driver took the boy's hand, and with his help, Beth settled him into a front seat beside his sister.

"You'll be fine, Bryce," she told him with a smile, and indeed, the boy did look less fearful now that he'd cleared the first hurdle. With that act of kindness, Beth's future was launched—not only as a high-school student, but also as a care provider.

The bus lurched into motion before Beth found a seat, and she quickly surveyed the students on board. A few of the faces were familiar—teens she had seen at miners' rallies on Labor Day—but no one greeted her. Perhaps they felt ill at ease, too. The first few seats were empty, but she moved farther back into the bus, hoping to find a friendly face.

One boy smiled, and said, "This seat is empty. You'd better take it. The bus will be full before we get to school."

"Thanks," Beth said, and as she sat beside him on the narrow seat, their shoulders touched, giving Beth a secure feeling.

"I saw you helping that little fellow onto the bus. Is he your brother?"

"No—I've never seen him before. I'm staying with my grandmother, and the children are her neighbors. He felt scared and needed a little help."

"That was nice of you." His words were simple but his appreciative glance conveyed much more. His brown eyes twinkled with love of life, and she liked his keen and serene expression. On that first day, she had noticed deep dimples in his cheeks when he smiled. He had a bronzed, lean face, with a firm mouth.

"This your first year in high school?" he asked.

"Yes, I could have gone last year, but my folks discouraged me. They didn't try to prevent it this year—maybe because I'm older."

"How old are you, anyway?"

"Fifteen, but I'll have a birthday in December. What grade are you in?"

"This is my senior year."

Though she could tell he was older than herself, Beth hadn't guessed he was a senior.

"What do you want to do when you finish?" she asked him.

"Go to work in the mines, I reckon," he replied. "My daddy is disabled, and the family has been sacrificing to let me finish high school. It'll be my turn to work now, and help my little sisters. By the way, my name is Clark Randolph."

Beth turned startled green eyes in his direction. A Randolph! *Just my luck,* she thought. When the bus slowed down to pick up other students, without speaking again, Beth moved to another seat, then stared out the window as the bus weaved in and out of the narrow streets of Harlan.

Why of all the places on this bus did she have to have sat beside a Randolph? If John Warner heard about it, that would be the end of her high-school days. For as long as she could remember, Beth had been taught that Warners and Randolphs were enemies. No one had ever spelled out why in so many words, but her father's shotgun was always loaded against the Randolphs, and it galled John Warner that he had to live in the shadow of Randolph Mountain.

By the time Beth had been born, hostilities were confined to fights at dances, or backing opposing candidates in elections, but from the tales she had heard, in the early days of the century, the feud had been a bloody one.

After World War II and the closure of many mines, most of the Warners and Randolphs had scattered to other vicinities, and there weren't many left in the mountains to carry on the feud. Still, John Warner continued to nurse the grudge and would cross the street rather than come face-to-face with any Randolph. So why did that cute, friendly boy have to be a Randolph?

When the bus stopped at the elementary school, Beth helped Bryce get down from the vehicle, and smiled when a waiting teacher took charge of the boy. "I'll help you off the bus tonight, Bryce, so don't worry," she called to him, and he waved shyly at her.

She'd been so caught up in Bryce's problem that she'd forgotten for a while the unknown awaiting her. She realized that she didn't have any idea where to go to enroll, so when the bus stopped at the high school she remained seated while the other students exited. When Clark passed by her, he paused, pointing, "You go through that door and turn to the right to reach the office. That's where you have to register." She nodded her thanks, and he motioned for her to precede him down the aisle.

As she moved toward the doors he had indicated, Clark said, "You didn't tell me your name."

"Beth Warner."

The distress in Clark's brown eyes was quickly replaced by laughter. "Oh, I see," he said knowingly. "That's too bad."

For the next two months, Beth was keenly aware of Clark as she boarded the bus each morning. If she met his gaze, he'd nod hello with a big smile. She'd nod back, but she carefully avoided any conversation with him. Occasionally, as he passed her seat, Clark would tug tenderly on her hair and lay his warm hand on her shoulder, but she ignored him. Her ears were always alert to any comment about Clark by her friends, and she had learned that he lived with his family in the Harlan school district, but that they also had a country home where they spent weekends and summers.

To her surprise, Beth did well academically in school, and soon had friends among girls who were much like her—those with very little money, from large families, and who received scant encouragement at home for furthering their education.

Beth made friends cautiously, but her shy, affectionate smile endeared her to teachers and students alike. That she seemed unaware of her rare beauty—which was accented by a firm little chin below even, white teeth, and a shapely mouth with full lips—made her peers take notice of her.

Beth was attentive in class and studied hard each night. She made above-average grades, for she considered that education was the only way to further

her dreams of leaving Kentucky. On Friday evenings, Beth's parents came to take her home and brought her back to Harlan on Monday mornings. Beth felt guilty when she realized how much her parents looked forward to seeing her each weekend. She understood that the house was bleak when she went away, and her conscience was troubled.

Besides her school studies, Beth was getting some practical experience in being a caregiver, for she had volunteered to spend several hours each night with Angie Reymond, an elderly friend of her grandmother who needed someone to stay with her while her daughter was at work. Angie's income was limited, and she could only afford to hire a person to stay during the day. Beth didn't mind sitting with the elderly woman because she could do her homework there as well as at her grandmother's home.

Several boys at school had noticed her, but none had captivated her thoughts like Clark. Each day on the bus, he continued to show interest in her but she continued to ignore him—not that she personally had any ill will toward the Randolphs, but she didn't want to irritate her father, whom she loved in spite of his prejudices.

One Saturday afternoon in late October, Beth was walking in the woods atop Randolph Mountain, unwilling to stay inside on such a beautiful day. Autumn was waning, and she wanted to enjoy the last vestiges of the season's beauty before a windy winter blast rolled down the mountain, bringing drabness and isolation.

She had been climbing steadily, and the afternoon

was warm, so Beth pulled off her jacket and leaned against a towering oak as she peered through the trees at the Cumberland River Valley to the west. A haze hung over the valley, but she could see the crowded, narrow streets of Harlan, and her school building in the middle of town.

"Hi, Beth Warner." The voice startled her, and she looked around wildly. She hadn't suspected that anyone else would be hiking today. "Look up. I'm in the tree."

Beth recognized his voice, and she looked upward to see Clark peering over the edge of a hunting platform, loftily perched in the branches of the large oak tree.

"Hi, Clark Randolph."

"Come on up," he said, indicating the homemade ladder attached to the tree. "The view is a lot better from up here."

"Warners don't talk to Randolphs."

"Why?"

"Why, what?"

"Why won't Warners talk to Randolphs?"

Beth thought for a while, and she laughed. "I don't have the least idea."

"Neither do I," Clark said. "Here, I'll give you a hand."

Throwing caution to the wind, Beth set her foot on the first rung of the ladder, thus charting her course along a path that had brought her pleasure and comfort, but which had also caused much of the grief and loneliness she was experiencing today. She hadn't thought of the long-range consequences that day, however.

With an outstretched hand, Clark was waiting to help her onto the platform where he knelt.

"What are you doing up here?" Beth asked, glancing around with interest.

"Looking into your pretty green eyes," he said.

"Oh, be serious. I mean, what were you doing before I came along?"

"Building a deer stand for hunting season. I had one down the mountain a ways, but it's crumbled into ruins." He pointed proudly to what he had already accomplished—a square platform built from rough lumber, with a miniature shack in the middle of it. "I built the little room to sit in if it's raining or snowing. Most of the time, I'll sit here on the platform and watch."

"Do you own this mountain?"

He laughed. "Mining companies own most of these woods, but some of the owners allow hunting."

"I never come in the woods during deer season."

"A good idea—it's too dangerous. But that's three weeks away. You can ramble around until then."

Beth sat beside Clark and they dangled their feet over the side of the platform.

"How are you getting along at school, Beth?"

"All right. I've been studying hard, and my grades for the first grading period were tops. My parents are really proud of me."

"I've heard how you've been sitting at night with Mrs. Reymond. Not many girls would give up their evenings to sit with an old lady. I hear she's kinda grouchy, too."

Beth laughed. "She is, but I'm used to grouchy old people. My daddy is grouchy with everyone except me. It's because they don't feel very well, so I just overlook it."

Clark's admiration for her was evident in his eyes. "You're a caring person, Beth. I admire that."

His candor embarrassed Beth, and she didn't know how to answer him, so she lifted a hand and brushed back her long hair nervously.

"I've been wanting to talk to you, Beth, but you acted like you didn't want anything to do with me."

"I was afraid to talk to you. My folks weren't too keen on my going to school in Harlan anyway, and I figured if Daddy heard I'd been talking to a Randolph, that would be a good excuse to take me out of school."

"So it wasn't that you didn't want to be friends?"

Beth shook her head, lowering her eyes.

With a gentle hand, Clark turned her head to face him. "Answer me, Bethie," his deep voice insisted.

"No, I liked you right from the start," she admitted, her gaze meeting his brown eyes unflinchingly. "Until I found out who you were."

"These old feuds are foolish, anyway," Clark said.

"I've never known what caused the trouble. Daddy always gets so angry when I ask him, I've stopped mentioning the Randolphs."

"Best I can figure out, the Warners and the Randolphs fought on different sides in the Civil War, and they wouldn't let their differences die when the war ended.''

"That's over a hundred years ago!"

"But it was a common situation in many border states where loyalties were divided. Even after the fighting ended, older people harped on the past and kept the bitterness stirred up.''

"Like my daddy," Beth said. "He doesn't have anything else to think about.''

"Then you will be my friend?" Clark persisted.

"If we can keep my family from finding out, but that won't be easy.''

"We can meet up here until it's really cold, and then we'll think of something else. I feel as if I just have to be with you, Beth. Something happened to my heart that first day when you got on the school bus, and I haven't been able to get you out of my thoughts since.''

Beth felt her face flushing, and she couldn't meet Clark's eyes, but she didn't resist when he took her hand in his. She didn't doubt the truth of Clark's words, for hadn't she felt the same? Some of her girlfriends would talk about crushes they had on boys. Some even believed they were in love. Beth had never felt that way about a boy. But the way she felt about Clark was different. All new. A giddy feeling, yet serious and even frightening. Did she *love* Clark? Was that what had happened to her?

She hoped not, because Clark Randolph was not the kind of person who could share her plans for the future. He intended to work in the coal mines as soon as he graduated from high school, and she never wanted to marry a miner.

"What about your family, Clark? Is your father a miner?"

"He used to be, but he was hurt in a slate fall when I was just a boy, and he's not been able to work since. I have two little sisters, and my mother takes care of all of us. She hasn't had an easy life, but you never hear her complaining. My daddy is a preacher now."

Clark looked upward at the colorful foliage and the white clouds floating by in a baby-blue sky, then sighed deeply. "Do you know what I think of when I'm out in the woods on a day like this? I think of God. What do you think of, Beth?"

"I don't think of God, that's for sure. I think of the beauty, I suppose."

"But God is the one who created all of this beauty that reminds me of the words of the psalmist David, 'The heavens declare the glory of God; and the firmament sheweth his handiwork.' How could you *not* think of God?"

Beth's legs were getting numb, and she inched away from the side of the platform to lean against the small structure. Clark moved close to her as a slight breeze scattered reddish-brown oak leaves over their shoulders.

"If your father is a preacher, then you probably hear a lot about God at your house, but my daddy doesn't hold with religion. The only time I ever hear God mentioned is when my half brothers are visiting. They cuss a lot, using God's name."

"But I want you to know the God I do, Bethie. I

can tell you're lonely and fearful lots of times. If you accept Jesus, God's son, into your heart, life will be a lot more peaceful for you.''

"Perhaps what you say is true, but when I've gotten this far without God, I don't figure I need Him now."

"Someday you'll change your mind. You'll want God really bad, and if you do, call out to Him. He will hear you.''

Clark's words were foreign to Beth, but because she liked to hear him talk, she listened, and for the first time, a tiny seed was planted in Beth's heart.

Chapter Two

Their secret friendship continued throughout the rest of the school year, and while their interest in each other must have been evident to their classmates, Beth's family didn't learn about it. They sat together on the bus occasionally, although they tried to be casual about it. Sometimes when he walked past her seat, Clark would drop a folded note into her lap. By spring she had accumulated many of them. Beth hid the notes in a shoe box beneath her bed. She wouldn't throw Clark's messages away, but if she didn't hide them, either her mother or grandmother was sure to find them.

Beth got out of bed and walked around the cold motel room, her eyes misting when she thought of those notes. She still had them in her possession, but she didn't need to read them anymore—the words of most of them were etched on her heart. As the sound of running water in the rooms beside hers signaled that morning had come, she remembered one of the messages he had given her: "You're looking mighty pretty this morning. The sun is shining on your hair, making it the color of autumn leaves. I dreamed about you last night, Bethie."

On the day before the schools closed for the Christmas holidays that year, Clark had slipped a note to her when they passed in the hallway.

His message was brief: "Try to come to the tree stand on Christmas Eve. I'll be there around noon."

Christmas had no particular significance for Beth's family, although some of her half siblings and their families usually came for the day. Beth had worked hard for two days helping her mother prepare for the meal, and Mrs. Warner had no objection when her daughter stated her intention of hiking for a few hours.

Beth suspected that Clark would bring her a present, and she wanted to buy something for him, but since her parents were sacrificing to pay her school expenses, she wouldn't use any of their scarce money to buy a gift for a Randolph. Before she left the house, she slipped one of her school pictures into her pocket.

The weather was mild for December, and Beth was panting hard and sweating profusely before she reached the tree house, where Clark was already waiting at the base of the tree. His brown eyes brightened when he saw her, and he pulled her into his arms—a liberty he hadn't taken before.

"Merry Christmas, Bethie," he whispered, and lowered his head to kiss her lips tenderly.

Breathless, Beth whispered, "It's my first kiss."

"Mine, too. You're the first girl I've ever wanted

to kiss," Clark said, and he bent over and kissed her again.

"See what I've been doing while I waited." He pointed to the trunk of a beech tree, where he had carved a large heart to enclose his initials and hers. "C.R. loves B.W.," he read proudly.

In an effort to slow the acceleration of her heartbeat, Beth said sternly, "I hope none of my family sees that."

Clark laughed. "Not likely that they will. It's cold and windy up on the platform. Let's walk around the mountain and find a spot in the sun."

Hand in hand, they wandered into the deeper woods, and Beth said, "I feel terrible sneaking around to meet you this way. There have been a few times I've been tempted to tell Mom, but I'm afraid she'll tell Daddy, and that would be the end of our friendship."

Clark squeezed the hand he held. "I've been praying for a way for us to be together always without keeping it a secret."

Beth grew tense as she always did when Clark mentioned the future.

"Do you ever think of leaving here?" she asked.

Clark stopped in midstride and turned to her in surprise. "'Leaving'? You don't mean—leave Kentucky?"

She nodded. "I want to go someplace else to live as soon as I graduate from high school. I don't suppose I'll have enough money to go to college, but I'm going to take secretarial courses during my last two years in school, and I should be able to find a job. I thought I could save some money and try to go to college at night.''

''What do you have against Kentucky?''

''I don't want to live as my parents have. And I can't see that my life will ever improve if I don't move away.''

They sat down at the entrance to a small cave where the sun shone directly on them. ''It seems we have different ideas about what the future holds for us,'' Clark said, disappointment evident in his voice.

Beth was sorry to have hurt Clark's feelings, but she had to be honest with him. ''I thought I should tell you.''

Clark drew a package from his pocket. ''This may not be the kind of gift you want, but even if we don't agree on the future, I know that you'll never be truly content unless you follow the way of life presented in this book. If you want to serve other people, the path starts here.''

Unsuspecting, Beth opened the package and found a Bible. Trying to stifle her disappointment, she murmured, ''Thank you,'' wondering why he thought she would want a Bible.

Beth had attended church with her grandmother a few times, so she had some basic knowledge about what the Bible was, but she'd never read it for herself, and it felt like a heavy weight lying in her hand and on her heart. Perhaps sensing this, Clark said, ''I hope you'll read it, and a good place to start would be the New Testament. A new way of life will open to you when you read these words.''

''I don't know, Clark,'' Beth said hesitantly.

"You do believe in God, don't you?"

"I haven't thought about it a lot."

"Promise me you'll read it."

He took the Bible from her hands and opened it. "Why not start with the Christmas story?" He turned to the second chapter of Luke. "'And it came to pass in those days, that there went out a decree from Caesar Augustus, that all the world should be taxed.'"

The reverence in his voice and the intent expression on his face disturbed Beth, and she quickly took the Bible from his hand.

"All right, I'll read it, but I have to go home now. I told Mom I wouldn't be gone very long. I'm worried about her, Clark. I think she's sick and won't tell me. I don't know what I'd do if anything happened to her. Daddy can't stay by himself, so I would probably have to quit school and stay home to take care of him. I love my parents, and I suppose my decision to be of service to others should start at home, but I can't bear the thoughts of being stuck in that hollow for the rest of my life."

Clark put his arm around her shoulders and pulled her close as they walked along the narrow trail. "I'll take care of you, Bethie."

Before they parted, Beth said, "I didn't know what to give you for Christmas, but I thought you might like this." She withdrew the photo of herself from her pocket and handed it to Clark.

His face lighted, and he kissed the photo. "You couldn't have given me anything to please me more. I wanted one of your pictures and thought of giving you one of mine, but I was afraid I'd get you into trouble."

"It's true that I can't have your photo around the house."

Clark pulled her into a tight embrace, and when he lowered his lips to hers, a new, strange emotion stirred in the deepest recesses of Beth's heart. Since it was strange, it was also frightening; but as Clark's kiss intensified, the tender, sweet feelings that swept over her seemed so wondrous and precious. *Was this love?* Would it persist, or would she awaken tomorrow wondering what had sparked this rare emotion?

Beth's arms were around Clark's neck when he lifted his lips, and she looked long into his eyes, trying to interpret what message they held for her, but Clark didn't leave her to wonder.

"I love you, Bethie. I have since the first day I saw you, and I'll love you until I die."

"How can you be so sure?" Beth murmured. "Lots of things could happen to turn your love from me."

"I guess I'm like Daddy. The minute he saw my mother, he knew she was the girl for him."

"I care for you, too, Clark. I think about you all the time when we're apart. But you know as well as I do, there's no future for us together."

He shook his head as if he wouldn't accept her decision, but she pulled away from him after placing a gentle kiss on his cheek.

As Beth walked down the mountain, she thought of what she had experienced when he'd kissed her. She didn't want to love Clark. She wanted to love a man who would take her away from Harlan County, and

Clark obviously wouldn't. Not that Beth had anything against Kentucky in general. She wouldn't mind living in Louisville or Lexington—she was just tired of Warner Hollow, and she wanted to get away from her half brothers, who were always in some kind of trouble with the law.

When she got home, Beth locked the Bible in a small cedar chest in her room, but that night after she undressed, she retrieved the Bible and took it into bed with her. The room was too cold for her to stay up for long, but she did open to the Gospel of Luke where Clark had told her to read. The account of the birth of Jesus was interesting, but it meant no more to her than a story she might read in a history book. As she leafed through the pages of the Bible, she noticed that Clark had underlined certain verses. She didn't read all of them, but one caught her eye, and she read aloud, "'Many waters cannot quench love, neither can the floods drown it: if a man would give all the substance of his house for love, it would be utterly contemned.'"

Was this another way Clark had of declaring his love for her?

Beth tucked the Bible under her pillow and turned out the light. As she snuggled under the heavy quilts, she thought of the two gifts Clark had given her today—his love and the Bible. Sleep would have come much more quickly if she hadn't been beset by the overwhelming certainty that her future happiness depended on the value she placed on those gifts.

As Beth dressed for the day she remembered that Christmas Eve long ago. She recalled how, in spite of her dreams of the future, she had never believed that she could achieve the goal she had now reached. Her good fortune had come about as a result of a scholarship. During her last year in high school, she had applied for and received a grant awarded annually by Shriver Mining Company for the orphan of a disabled miner.

The grant had guaranteed funds for a five-year curriculum or less, depending upon the choice of careers. It provided for tuition, books, housing, food, and a transportation allowance. The recipient of the scholarship would matriculate at a college in eastern Pennsylvania that was heavily endowed by Shriver Mining Company, and she could choose from a variety of vocations, most of them specifically planned for service in the coalfields. All of this had sounded fine until Beth came to the last few lines.

This scholarship is conditional upon the willingness of the recipient, after graduation, to return to Kentucky and work for two years in the coalmining region, using her training for the good of the people in the area. The recipient will be compensated by the prevailing wage at that time in the profession she has chosen.

Beth's disappointment had been as keen as a knife wound when she'd read that stipulation, for she had considered the scholarship a ticket to a life outside Kentucky, and momentarily, she had considered rejecting it, but would she ever have a better opportunity for advancement? Probably not.

There had been no money from any other source. She had accepted the scholarship, and latently remembering her dream to be a second Florence Nightingale, had registered in a five-year program that would qualify her as an advanced registered nurse-practitioner. She'd completed her training in four and a half years by taking classes at night and during summer sessions. She had also worked for a year, at a minimal wage, in the maternity department of a local hospital in order to be certified in midwifery. Her strenuous schedule had left her no free time, and she hadn't been back to Kentucky since she'd left.

In fact, she hadn't wanted to come back even now. But she had committed herself, and she had an eleven o'clock appointment in Lexington with Milton Shriver, CEO of Shriver Mining Company. As she accessed I-75, heading north, a glance at her watch showed that she had two hours remaining until then.

No wonder Shriver Mining could afford to pay my way through college, Beth thought when she drove into the company's paved parking lot and found an empty spot reserved for visitors. The four-story brick building had been built ten years ago, she noted on the cornerstone. If she could work here, perhaps her two years of service, which she had been dreading like a prison sentence, might not be too bad.

Beth was a little worried about her appearance, for her wardrobe was limited. She had dressed this morning in a gray wool suit she'd found at a thrift shop. It looked nearly new and the classic tailored style didn't look totally out of fashion. She wore it with a green blouse that enhanced her eyes, and had added the pearl necklace and earrings that had been a high-school graduation gift from her grandmother. She had applied makeup sparingly except for an extra dab of foundation below her eyes, which were weary from lack of sleep.

As Beth entered the building, her small supple body was mirrored in the gleaming front door, and she appraised her appearance. She couldn't afford anything better, but overall her outfit looked fashionable.

"I have an appointment with Milton Shriver," she said to the receptionist, in a voice that trembled slightly.

"Your name?" the woman inquired, looking Beth over curiously, making her wonder if the receptionist could tell she was wearing secondhand clothing.

"Beth Warner."

The woman spoke into the intercom. "Beth Warner to see you, Mr. Shriver."

"Please show her to my office," a deep voice answered.

"This way," the tall, well-proportioned woman said, leaving her chair with one fluid movement and indicating that Beth should follow her. Their footsteps made no noise on the thick carpet as they moved down the hallway, the walls of which were lined with portraits of past company officials.

The receptionist opened the door into a large room decorated with framed black-and-white photos of mining activities in an earlier period, and said, "This is Mr. Shriver, Miss Warner," and motioned Beth inside.

A portly, graying man, probably in his sixties,

Shriver left his desk and came to greet Beth. "It's a pleasure to meet you at last, Miss Warner. I had hoped that you would pay us a visit before this."

"I didn't have any time for visiting. I kept to a heavy schedule so that I could finish my training early. Besides, Grandmother Blaine, my guardian, died the summer I went away to college, and I didn't have any other ties here. This is the first time I've returned to Kentucky since I went away to college."

Seating Beth in a chair near his desk, Shriver said, "We're pleased with your college record. It's customary for the director of student affairs at the college to give us an annual report on the progress of our scholarship recipients. You're to be congratulated for your achievements."

Beth accepted his praise with a nod. "I owed it to Shriver Mining to learn as much as possible. I appreciate winning the scholarship—I could never have gone to college without it. And now, what am I to do for the next two years?"

Shriver smiled. "We hope that you will consider working many years for our firm, but after two years, you are free to make your own decision." He intertwined his fingers as he contemplated. "We were pleased when you chose the nursing profession, because one of our greatest concerns is the health of our miners and their families. And there's a trend in our area for women to prefer home birthing, so your training in midwifery was an excellent choice."

"My paternal grandmother was a rather famous midwife, and I may have inherited the desire to follow in her footsteps."

"We're currently launching a program of health care and are anticipating your help in getting it started out. We plan to establish an outpatient clinic—which we want you to organize and manage—with a major focus on service to women and children. Our miners' families can come there, at minimal cost, for their health needs. And you would also be available for assisting at home births if the women prefer that."

"There wouldn't be a doctor at the clinic?"

"Yes, in a supervisory role. Wesley Andrews, a notable doctor in the area, would be at the clinic a few hours each week, but you will take part of the heavy load he carries by monitoring blood pressure and similar problems, giving immunization shots, and treating colds and flu. But maternity care will be your major focus, with prenatal and postnatal instruction as you can fit those classes into your schedule. Later on, if this proves successful, we will build other clinics. This will be a pilot project, and your success will greatly influence our plans for expansion. What do you think?"

She stared at the man for a few minutes—incredulous that he would expect one person to do all that work. And a person with so little professional experience, besides.

"It sounds rather overwhelming, but I'm hardly in a position to refuse," she replied honestly.

Shriver laughed lightly. "I'll admit I would be disappointed if you refused this assignment, but I also know that if you aren't willing, aren't excited about the project, it won't be successful."

"Of course, I'll accept it and do the best I can. It

sounds as if it could be a great benefit to the miners and their families. Where's the clinic located?''

"Near Shriver Mine No. 10 in Harlan County."

Beth clutched the arms of the chair as dizziness swept over her, and the face of Milton Shriver faded before her eyes.

"What's the matter?" he asked, as he rose to assist her. "Are you ill?"

She waved him back to his chair, swallowed with difficulty, and tried to force a smile. "You gave me quite a shock. I was born in Harlan County and lived there until I was sixteen years old. Memories of my childhood aren't pleasant, and I'd hoped that I would never have to live there again."

Shriver's face showed his surprise. "When you graduated from high school in Prestonburg, we naturally assumed that was your home. I didn't know that you had any connection to Harlan County."

"It's been home to the Warners for over two hundred years, but I moved to Prestonburg with my maternal grandmother after the death of my parents."

"Under these circumstances," he replied kindly, "I won't hold you to your agreement to take over the clinic, but I would like for you to take a week to look over the situation before you reject it completely. I'll have one of our executives accompany you to Harlan County and show you the clinic and the area where you would work. He's an expert on conditions in the coalfields of eastern Kentucky. Just a minute, I'll have him come in—he's planning to take you to lunch."

Shriver walked to a door that opened into an adjoining office.

"Will you come in now, please?" A man then appeared in the open doorway, and at first, Beth didn't recognize him; he looked so different from the man she had once known.

"Beth, I want you to meet Clark Randolph, although Clark tells me that you're already acquainted. Clark will be your supervisor—your contact with the company."

Again, dizziness assailed Beth, but she struggled to her feet, wanting to run away, and the face she had once known so well blurred before her. This couldn't be Clark—no longer a miner, but a well-groomed executive, dressed in a dark business suit, silk tie, and white shirt, looking right at home in the headquarters of Shriver Mining Company.

But when he walked toward her, she knew it was Clark. Clothes couldn't change his graceful, easy tread, and his steady and serene gaze, which held her spellbound when he held out his hand. "Hello, Beth."

"Hello," she squeaked, and her voice sounded unnatural. Desperately needing some link to steady her nerves, she gripped his hand tightly, and even in the trauma of the moment, she noticed that his hands were not rough to the touch as they had been the last time she'd seen him.

Why had she ever come back to Kentucky? If she had taken a job elsewhere, she could eventually have repaid Shriver Mining the amount of the scholarship.

Milton Shriver looked from one to the other, his eyes keen question marks. Try as she would, Beth could not control her emotions. Clark had expected to see her, and he seemed to be at ease. In such a short time, how could Clark have progressed from an underground miner to the position he held here? Beth felt as if her face had a plaster cast over it, and she could hardly move her lips when she turned to Shriver.

"When do you want to see me again?"

"This afternoon or tomorrow, after you and Clark have had an opportunity to talk over your work."

"I guess I'll need to check into a motel if I'm going to be here a few days."

"That will be at our expense, Miss Warner. Clark will take care of it for you."

"Thank you." Without looking at Clark, Beth turned and walked out into the hall, but she could hear his footsteps behind her, and when they reached the front office, he said to the receptionist, "Stephanie, I'll be out of the office for a few hours." The woman favored Beth with a sharp glance, and Beth wondered if Stephanie could sense the tension between herself and Clark.

Clark opened the door for Beth, then took her arm as they went down the steps. Her nerves tightened at his touch.

"We'll go in my car," he said, and he led her to a red sport-utility vehicle, which had Shriver Mining Company emblazoned on the door. When she stepped inside, the last vestige of control to which she had so tenaciously held, deserted her, and she dropped her head on the padded dashboard and sobbed—hard, wrenching sobs that shook her entire body. As far as Beth could remember, she hadn't cried since she'd left Kentucky, but now she couldn't stop as she sobbed out the frustrations and disappointments of a lifetime.

Clark remained silent, though from time to time she felt his strong hand tenderly touch her shoulder or stroke her hair.

Last night, she had determined to forget the past, but as Clark drove quietly out of the parking lot and accessed Interstate 64 heading east, Beth's thoughts turned to the tumultuous incidents that had taken her away from Warner Hollow.

After the Christmas when Clark had declared his love for her, eastern Kentucky had been plunged into two months of inclement weather that closed the schools for weeks, and when they reopened, Beth was marooned at her home in Warner Hollow for an additional two weeks.

Consequently, she fell behind in her studies and her grades weren't nearly as good as they had been the first semester. She rarely saw Clark. They exchanged a few words on the school bus and passed an occasional note, but there was no opportunity to discuss what had happened between them on Christmas Eve.

When spring came, Clark signed up for the softball team, and he practiced after school and played on Saturdays. He took his father's car to school so he could have transportation home after ball practice, so he didn't often ride the bus.

One Friday afternoon in late April, however, Clark boarded the bus, and he sat beside Beth and slipped a note into her hand. She secreted the note in the pocket of her jacket, but she went to her bedroom as soon as she could and read his words: "Meet me at the tree stand, Sunday afternoon."

Beth was excited to have the opportunity to see Clark again, and she thought about it constantly until it was time to meet him. She hurried up the mountain, and she was panting when she reached their rendez-vous, disappointed to find that she was there ahead of Clark.

He came before too long, apologizing. "We were late getting home from church this morning, and we have another meeting tonight, so I can't stay long." He drew her into his arms. "I've missed you."

"Same here. I thought the winter would never end."

They climbed the ladder and sat on the platform. The sun shining through the tree branches showing the first signs of foliage was warm and relaxing.

"Looks as if the squirrels used our place as a kitchen table this winter," Clark said as he brushed acorn hulls and hickory-nut shells from the wide boards.

He sat beside her, with his arm around her shoulder, and Beth leaned against him.

"Beth, will you go to the prom with me?"

She drew a quick breath. "Oh, I wouldn't dare. It might start the feud again."

"Who's left to fight? Hardly any Randolphs live around here except my family, and we aren't going to be involved in a feud."

"My half brothers would pick a fight with anyone. As you may have gathered, I'm not very proud of my relatives. My sister, Luellen, doesn't like me, and the two boys are always in some kind of trouble. They would sue you in a minute if they thought they could make any money off you.''

"We don't have any money, so I'll risk it. Will you go with me?''

"Let me think about it.''

Wanting very much to attend the prom, Beth asked her mother for her permission, omitting the fact that freshmen couldn't go unless they went with an upperclassman.

"You'd need a new dress, I reckon.''

Her heart lightening, Beth said, ''I can send a letter to Pam, and she could pick out something suitable at that secondhand store. I've gotten through this year with the clothes she helped me to buy. She'll know what I need, and it won't cost much.''

Beth felt guilty deceiving her parents, but she didn't once lie to them—she just didn't tell them everything. She'd told her grandmother, though, that she wanted to go to the prom with Clark Randolph, and Ella had replied, ''Why not? Why should you be punished for what happened more than a hundred years ago? Besides, I know the Randolphs—they're good people and their son is a fine boy. Go and enjoy yourself.''

Pam mailed Beth an ankle-length white chiffon party dress, decorated with pearls on the bodice and neckline. It looked like new, as if it hadn't been worn more than once. Beth's mother was not demonstrative about her affection, but Beth knew that she was proud of her daughter's looks, and she insisted that Beth have a new pair of shoes. So Beth bought a pair of white low-heeled sling pumps, and she was pleased with her appearance as she dressed for the prom.

When Clark came to pick her up, he brought her a corsage of pink carnations. He was dressed in a new blue suit, white shirt, and tie, and Beth admired his sturdy and finely made body, both wiry and strong. She had never seen him in dress clothes before, and she thought what a pity that he wouldn't choose a profession in which he could appear so dashing all the time.

Neither Beth nor Clark knew how to dance, but they enjoyed listening to the music and watching the others. She had a good time, and it was an evening to remember, but when the prom was over, instead of driving back to her grandmother's house, Clark drove along the highway for several miles. When he turned onto a secondary road, Beth gave him a quick look.

"Where are you going?"

"Beth, I won't keep you out late, but I want to talk to you."

After he parked the car, he put his arms around Beth, and he didn't keep her in doubt about his intentions.

"I've told you that I love you, and now I want to propose. I want to marry you, Beth. I'm going to work in the mines next month, and I'll be making good money. I can support a wife, as well as help out my family."

Beth's heart beat like a drum. The thought of marriage to Clark seemed like a happy dream. A dream that could actually come true. But she was determined that her mind, rather than her heart, would rule her. She moved away from him.

"Clark, I don't want to get married. I've finally gotten my parents to agree to send me to high school, and I want to go to college if I can find a way. Besides, I'm only sixteen."

"Lots of girls marry at sixteen, and you could still go to school," he insisted. "We can live with my parents."

"Live with your parents! What kind of life would that be?"

"I'll need to help support my family, and it will be easier if we're all under the same roof. Besides, if you're going to school, you wouldn't have time to take care of a house, and Mother wouldn't mind."

She put her hand over his mouth to stop his words, and he nibbled her fingers.

Steeling herself to ignore his caress, she said, "Clark, listen to me.... I don't want to hurt you, but I tried to tell you once before. I'm not interested in marrying anyone right now, but when I do marry, it won't be to a coal miner. I want to marry someone who will take me away from that kind of life—the fear of cave-ins like the one that disabled your father, the danger of diseases caused by being underground so much, the dread of losing your husband in a mine disaster. It's a hard life."

Beth hadn't noticed any stubbornness in Clark before, but he wouldn't take no for an answer this time.

"If you loved me, you'd be willing to accept my way of life."

"That's another way we differ. Most people I know believe it's a woman's duty to sacrifice every personal aspiration for the man in her life. I'm not willing to do that. My mother asked me once why I couldn't be like the other girls in our neighborhood, and I told her I didn't know. I still don't know why I'm different, but I am. And you know how much I want to have a profession of my own. Besides," she continued, "I haven't told you that I love you."

"But you do, don't you?"

"I probably do," she admitted quietly. His brown eyes gazing into her own shone with a hopeful light. But it was quickly extinguished when she added, "But I don't see that loving you changes anything for me, Clark. I'm sorry."

Without another word, Clark turned the car around and started back toward town. Beth longed to erase the misery reflected on his face, but she doubted that his pain was any worse than the agony in her own heart. Regardless of how much it hurt, she couldn't do what he wanted.

When he stopped in front of the Blaine home, Clark took her hand and said, "I'm not mad at you, Bethie— only sorry that you don't love me as much as I love you."

"Let me ask you a question, Clark. You think I don't love you because I won't marry you and settle down in Harlan County for the rest of my life. If I married you, would you leave Kentucky and go with me to live in some other state?"

His startled brown eyes met hers, luminous in the glow of the streetlight. "I hadn't thought of it that way. I can't go away and leave my family without some help. I have an obligation to them."

"Then we're at an impasse."

"Where do we go from here?"

"You know the answer as well as I do, Clark."

"You mean we should stop seeing each other?"

"What else? Why keep turning a knife that will only cause deeper pain?"

"It will break my heart, but I'll do what you say."

"We won't be seeing each other much now anyway, since you won't be going to school."

"We could meet on the mountain now that spring has come," he said hopefully.

Beth shook her head, and Clark drew her into his arms and drained the depth of his despair onto her lips. "I thought this was going to be the happiest night of my life," he said. "Instead, it's the blackest."

Beth held him tightly for a moment, savoring his closeness, then slipped out of his arms, and seemingly out of his life. With brimming eyes, she jumped from the car and ran up the steps and into the house.

Beth was startled when a horn sounded behind them, and realizing that Clark was driving more slowly, she lifted her head as he exited the interstate onto a secondary road.

"Please excuse my behavior, Clark," she said. "Now that I'm back in Kentucky, I keep remembering incidents of the past I thought I'd forgotten completely. Believe me, I'm not usually so weepy."

She sensed that Clark was grinning, although she wouldn't look directly at him.

"I've never thought of you as a crybaby, but you've had plenty of reason to cry."

"I've been thinking about the night I went with you to the prom."

"I've thought of that lots of times, too. You sure were pretty in that white dress."

"The pink corsage made it look nicer. You were so handsome in your new suit, and I was happy to be your date." She sniffed. "I'm sorry the night had to end on a sour note."

Clark patted her hands where they lay clenched in her lap. "That's the way it should have been, so don't worry about it. We can't do anything about the past."

Beth sighed, and cupped her fingers around his. "The rest of that year was the worst time of my life."

"I know, and I wish I could have helped you more. I thought my heart would break when you moved away."

Beth's thoughts drifted back to the dismal closing days of her freshman year. Those were heartrending days without Clark's attention—days that were only a prelude to what the summer held for Beth. In mid-June her mother had a heart attack and died before an ambulance could reach the hollow; and moments after John Warner realized that his wife was dead, he slumped in his rocking chair and, gasping for breath, also died.

For the two days prior to the funeral, Beth wandered around in a state of shock. Her half siblings flocked into the house, took over burial arrangements, insisting that the property belonged to them now; and legally it did, because John had deeded the property to his first wife before he'd joined the army during World War II. Beth had no desire to own the property, but she did need a home.

That problem was solved when Ella Blaine arrived

at the house and said, "Pack your things, Beth, and as soon as the funeral is over, I'm taking you to live with me all the time." Ella took a long look at the coffin of her youngest daughter. "But we won't stay in Harlan County. There are too many bad memories for both of us here. I'm going to sell out and move to Prestonburg where my other children live—I only stayed here to be close to Mary." Beth was heartened by that news, especially since Pam and Ray Gordon had also moved to Prestonburg, and at that distance, she would be rid of her half siblings, and unlikely to see Clark at all, although she did wish she could see him once more before she left the area.

Quite a large gathering of neighbors and family came to the funeral, most of them arriving a day early so they could participate in the double wake. When Beth followed the funeral procession out of the house, she saw Clark standing to one side, his brown eyes full of compassion. It was unheard of for a Randolph to attend a Warner funeral, and it must have taken a lot of courage to risk the hostility that would ensue if he were recognized.

After the graveside service, Beth looked around to see if Clark had gone. He was standing apart from the others, and she walked to his side.

He reached out and took her hand. "I'm sorry, Bethie."

At first her throat was too tight for speech. Clark lifted a hand and wiped away the tears that ran down her cheeks, and his touch was rough on her face. That's what the coal mines do to you, she thought bitterly. Only a month in the mine, and already, his hands were rough and scruffy.

"I'm leaving right away, Clark, to live with my grandmother. I'll finish high school in Prestonburg."

"The mountains are going to seem mighty empty without you, but I can see that it's best for you to leave. Will I ever see you again?"

"I don't know."

After the shock of her parents' tragic deaths had worn off, Beth had enjoyed living in Prestonburg. She'd made new friends, and her grades were above average. At times her wayward thoughts turned to Clark and the love they had known, but, with determination, she pushed the memories aside. She liked living near Pam Gordon, and she spent a lot of time at the Gordons' house, especially when Ray was touring with his band.

Thinking of her friend, Beth said, "I stopped by Prestonburg to see Pam a couple of days ago, and learned they'd moved. Do you see Ray and Pam often?"

"Not as much as I did before I came to Lexington. Haven't you kept in touch with Pam?"

Shaking her head, Beth said, "No, and I'm ashamed to admit it. As good as Pam was to help me when I was in high school, I should at least have sent her a Christmas card. I thought I was better off to forget people in Kentucky, but I'm beginning to have second thoughts about it."

Yes, Pam had helped her buy clothes and supported her in everything she wanted to do, but they couldn't agree about Beth's friendship with Alex.

In the closing months of her senior year, her life changed completely when she met Alex Connor.

Alex was associated with the United States Foreign Service, and was in Kentucky to determine how the state's products, particularly coal and tobacco, could be expanded into overseas markets. He had a temporary office in Prestonburg, and Beth was assigned to work there a few hours each week to fulfill the requirements of her business-cooperative course, whereby high-school seniors gained work experience in local businesses.

Alex seemed the embodiment of Beth's dreams. He was educated, he was handsome—blond-haired, blue-eyed, with a lean build—and he appeared to be captivated by Beth. They had several dates, and Beth soon found out that his aspirations matched hers. Her dream of reaching beyond Kentucky soared when she was with Alex.

"A few more years of drudgery like this," he often said, "and I'll have enough years of service to be transferred overseas. I want to see the world."

On her graduation night, when Beth received the scholarship, her excitement was boundless, especially since she had a date with Alex and some other graduates for a gala dinner after the ceremonies. Beth thought she was well on her way toward her coveted goal, until she came face-to-face with Clark Randolph at the close of the graduation exercises.

He approached her, smiling, and because her heart raced at the sight of this man, whom she hadn't seen since she'd left Harlan County, she was less friendly with him than she might otherwise have been. She was looking toward the future now—she could spare no thoughts on the past. Why did he have to show up now and remind her of what she'd given up?

"Congratulations, Bethie," he said. "I wanted to see you graduate."

"But how did you know?"

"Ray Gordon and I are friends. I ask him how you are and what you're up to."

Had Ray told Clark that she'd been dating Alex?

"He's never mentioned your name to me."

"I figured you didn't want to hear about me, so I asked him not to say anything."

Apparently Clark had come straight from the coal mine because he was dressed in jeans that were none too clean, and his brown hair was long and tousled. His hands still had the sheen of coal on them. Looking over Clark's shoulder, Beth saw Alex heading in her direction. She just couldn't introduce him to Clark, who reminded her of things she was determined to forget.

"Thanks for coming, Clark. Now, if you'll excuse me, I've made plans for a graduation party."

Perhaps it wasn't only her words, but the careless, unfeeling way she had spoken, that made Clark gasp, and left Beth with a memory of the hurt, reproachful look in his brown eyes that had haunted her dreams and waking hours for years afterward. The evening that she had anticipated with so much pleasure turned into a great disappointment, and even now she couldn't look back on it without inward agony. Coming on the heels of her humiliating treatment of Clark, Alex had told her that he had been assigned to overseas duty, making it obvious that he didn't intend to make any commitment to her. But the crushing blow of the evening came when she looked more closely at the scholarship she'd been awarded and found that she would be obligated to return to Kentucky after she received her college degree.

Chapter Three

B eth was startled when Clark laid his hand on her shoulder. "Beth, are you feeling any better yet?"

With difficulty, she returned to the present and shook her head.

He reached for his cell phone and dialed.

"Stephanie, this is Clark. Please tell Mr. Shriver that Miss Warner and I will not return to the office this afternoon. She will see him tomorrow morning."

He dialed again. "This is Clark Randolph, Shriver Mining Company. Please make a reservation for the next two nights for Beth Warner, at our expense. She will check in later on this evening."

After he finished his phone calls, Clark drove for several miles in silence. "Beth," he said at last, "we must go somewhere and talk. We can go to a restaurant but it won't be very private. Do you have any objections to going to my apartment?"

"Your apartment will be fine. I'm too upset to be seen in public right now."

Clark turned the vehicle and started toward Lexington. Beth looked out the window rather than face him. When he entered the parking garage of a high-rise apartment building, she needed no more proof that Clark's economic situation had improved greatly. She had refused to marry him because she wanted someone to take her away from eastern Kentucky, and now here he was, ensconced in a city, and she was going back to Harlan County. Beth could have cried over the ironic twist of fate, but she didn't have any more tears left. She'd shed them all in his luxury vehicle.

"I live on the eighth floor," he said. "I like it up there. I can look out over most of the other buildings and pretend I see the mountains, even if I can't."

"Then you don't like living here?" Beth asked in some surprise, as they entered the heavily carpeted building and waited for the elevator.

"It isn't home."

Beth hadn't looked at Clark since she'd first seen him in Shriver's office, but she sensed that his tender, compassionate eyes watched her intently.

"It's just a small apartment," he said, as he opened the door into a combination living room and kitchenette, with a door to the left leading to a bedroom. Clark took her coat and hung it in the closet, then shrugged out of his topcoat.

"I'll make something to drink. Tea or coffee?"

"Tea with some sugar, please. If I may, I'll go to the bathroom and rinse my face."

He pointed toward the bedroom door, turned on the gas burner, and ran water into a teakettle. Beth took her purse and went into the bathroom. Her makeup was streaked, her eyes were red, and her skin felt dry and parched. She drenched a washcloth with hot water and soaked up the warmth from it into her face. With the small amount of makeup she had in her purse, she was able to repair some of the damage from her crying jag.

As she walked through Clark's bedroom, she stopped abruptly and stared at the picture in a gilded heart-shaped frame on the nightstand beside his bed. It was her ninth-grade picture—the one she had once given him for Christmas. Beth clutched her throat, hardly able to breathe, and a sob escaped her lips. "Oh, Clark," she whispered.

So Clark was still harboring the unfailing love he'd once declared for her. She had assumed that by now he had found someone else. Dared she admit that she had feared he might have forgotten her? And she certainly wouldn't have blamed him if he had.

Returning to the kitchen, she found Clark had set two cups and two small plates on the table. Water was boiling, and she smelled scrambled eggs and toast. She didn't mention the picture.

He held a chair for her, put a tea bag in her cup and poured hot water over it. He placed a slice of toast and a portion of eggs on each plate, then pushed the butter plate to where she could reach it.

"Do you realize that this is the first time we've ever eaten a meal together?" he asked.

She lowered her eyes and fiddled with the spoon beside her plate.

"Sorry I can't do any better with the menu, but I

don't eat here except for breakfast. I'm either at a business dinner or bring in takeout.''

Beth could tell that Clark was chatting to give her time to regain her composure, but at last he said, ''I'm sorry that meeting me gave you such a jolt. I didn't realize it would be a complete surprise to you.''

''It wasn't only that. I've been wallowing in sentiment for the past two days, and encountering you was just the last straw. You see, I made the mistake yesterday of going back to Randolph Mountain, and all the memories that I'd kept bottled up for seven years exploded.''

''Do you want to talk about it?''

She shook her head. ''I'd rather hear about you. The last time I saw you, you were working in the mine. Today, you're an executive in the company. How did it happen?''

''I thought perhaps you'd heard.''

''Nothing. My grandmother died a few weeks before I went to Pennsylvania, and I didn't correspond with anyone in Kentucky while I was away.''

They ate in silence. Beth felt ill at ease in Clark's presence, and she had never been that way before. It was a strange sensation.

''Let's take our tea into the living room where we can be more comfortable.'' He poured some more hot water into their cups, replaced the tea bags in the liquid, and carried them to a table in front of the couch. She sat on the couch, and he took the chair opposite her.

''Didn't you know that my mother's maiden name was Shriver?''

Beth shook her head, wonderingly. The way he had occupied her mind for seven years, it was amazing how little she knew about him and his family.

"She's Milton Shriver's sister, but her father disowned her when she married Daddy, who was a poor coal miner. My mother is proud, and she never contacted any of her family—not even after Daddy was hurt and we lived in dire circumstances. Nor was she notified when her parents died."

Sometimes when Beth heard about the problems of others, she wondered if her childhood had been as difficult as she'd thought.

"Soon after you left for college, I was able to prevent a mine accident that could easily have led to a disaster involving the loss of many lives. The newspapers played up the story, and several of the company officials, including Milton, came down to the mine to thank me."

The hot tea was soothing and Beth kicked off her shoes, curled her feet beneath her, and listened wonderingly as Clark explained his rise from "rags to riches."

"After my grandfather died, Milton had become the CEO of the company, and when he realized my identity, he decided that it was time to make some recompense for the wrongs of the past. My parents refused to take anything from him, but he offered to send me to college and continue my salary, so that I could still help my family. It seemed like too good an opportunity to refuse."

Beth stared at him, her eyes wide in wonder. It

sounded like a fairy story, but it couldn't have happened to a more deserving person.

"While I was in college, I was an apprentice here at the corporate offices and out in the field, learning more about the mining industry. After two years I started to work full-time for the company, but I still take night classes and will eventually earn an engineering degree."

"What do you do for the company?"

"They've given me the title of 'technical supervisor,' but I'm mostly a troubleshooter," he said, with a grin. "It took a lot of doing to transform me from a miner to an executive, but the company enrolled me in some classes, so I've learned how to dress and how to conduct myself in various social situations."

She smiled at him. "I'm really impressed by your success. I was considering the irony of life a few minutes ago. You were content to stay in the coalfields, and now you're here in Lexington, living in a plush apartment and headed for the top. And I, who wanted to leave Kentucky forever, am being sent back to Harlan County. That news is what really set me off."

"I don't spend all my time in the office," he told her. "I'm around the coal mines more than I am here. That's why Milton thought I was the one to show you the new clinic and acquaint you with your work there."

"He said you would be my supervisor."

"Not really. I couldn't supervise a nurse, but I'm your liaison with the company. If you have any trouble, I'm supposed to assist you."

Beth put her cup on the table and walked to the window, where Clark had said he stood and pretended he was in the mountains. She found she couldn't imagine anything beyond the rooftops of the buildings around them and the noise of traffic that moved in a steady stream around the apartment complex. The cold air radiating from the windowpane reminded her of her chilly, miserable experience of the day before.

"I drove up Randolph Mountain yesterday, walked out to the summit, looked over my birthplace, and now I wish that I hadn't. For years I've tried to ignore that part of my life, but when I stood on the ridge with the wind sweeping up from the hollow, I started remembering things I hoped I'd forgotten. I've been miserable ever since."

Clark came to her side and put an arm around her shoulders. She leaned against him gratefully.

"Everything wasn't so bad, was it? Don't you have any pleasant memories?"

"No, not really, for my parents seemed to fear any changes in our lives, and I resented it. I know now that it was fear of the complications of ill health, but as a child, I didn't realize that. I was a misfit somehow—I was never satisfied with my life, but I couldn't seem to do anything about it. When I return to Harlan County, it will seem as if I'm retracing the past."

"You don't have to go back. Milton will find some other place for you—he's a reasonable man. People with your training are in demand in many different institutions." He paused for a moment, and his hand massaged her shoulders, and the muscles in her neck relaxed. "But, Bethie—" and her heart ached when he used his special name for her ''—if you're ever going to be happy, you'll have to deal with the past and the hang-ups you have about it. If you do choose to take this job, I'll be there to help you as much as possible. I'll see you over the rough spots.''

Wearily she said, ''Oh, I'll go—I don't think it's right to refuse or ask for a different assignment. If it hadn't been for Shriver Mining, I would probably be working for minimum wage in some store or market. I could never have gotten anyplace on my own. I owe the corporation two years of my life, but I dread it.''

Clark squeezed her slightly. ''Shall we go get your car and check you into the motel, then we can drive someplace for dinner? I know a nice restaurant close to the interstate a few miles to the west.''

''I do feel hungry. My stomach was in knots a few hours ago, but I'm getting over it.'' She touched his arm as they started to leave the apartment. ''I want you to know that I'm happy you've done so well, Clark. I'm proud of you, and thanks for understanding about what happened today. I don't know what Mr. Shriver thought of my behavior.''

''Whatever he thought, he won't question you about it. I've learned to have a great deal of respect for him.''

When they parked at the motel, Beth said, ''All I need for the night is that small case and the hanging bag that contains my better clothing. All of those other cartons are books and mementos I accumulated while I was away.''

''Nice car,'' Clark said, looking over the brown four-door sedan.

"It took almost all of the money I had to make a down payment on it, but I knew I had to have some kind of transportation. I've had it only about a week."

"You'll be getting an adequate salary now, so you won't have to worry about finances."

Clark carried in her luggage, and after Beth registered, he paid for her lodging with a company credit card.

"She may want to stay longer," he explained to the clerk, "but her plans are indefinite just yet."

In the room, Beth said, "Give me a few minutes to change my clothes." She took a dress from her garment bag, and carried the small suitcase to the bathroom. Clark flipped on the television, and when she returned, he was sprawled in the easy chair, engrossed in a football game.

"I always wanted to play football," he said. "That's one of the regrets of my past."

"Do you have many of them?" Beth asked, as she perched on the arm of the couch.

"Not many," he replied, and his face had a guarded look that didn't reveal his true thoughts.

"Are you sorry you went to work in the mine?"

"I'm not sorry I had a job where I could help my family, and if I hadn't gone to work as a miner, I wouldn't have the job I have today. But it doesn't seem as if I've ever had a chance to be 'young.' It would have been nice to have a few carefree years. I'm grateful to Milton for providing college for me, but I didn't have any time to enjoy life as a full-time student since I was in training at the firm while I went to school. The socializing and activities, like going out for a team, I mean."

"You've never had the chance to have much fun."

"I guess that's it. But you haven't either, have you?"

"No."

"Maybe it isn't too late for us. We're both out of school now—perhaps we can start enjoying life together."

Beth wouldn't look at him; she wasn't really sure of his meaning. "I'm not looking forward to much free time during the next two years."

"Why not? You won't have to work all the time." He reached for the remote and turned off the television. "Shall we go for dinner now?"

He stood and stretched, and Beth's heart stirred with so much yearning that she caught her breath. He was a man now, and an admirable one, yet he hadn't lost the boyish qualities that had drawn her to him in the first place—impulsiveness, simplicity, and compassion. She remembered vividly the night he had asked her to marry him. If she had said yes, she would now have all the material things she'd considered important, and which she'd thought marriage to Clark wouldn't provide. How wrong she had been! If she had the opportunity to live her life over, would she have made a different choice?

She lifted a shaking hand to smooth back her hair, and when she made no effort to leave the room, Clark came to her and clasped her trembling fingers. He lifted her chin with his other hand. "What are you thinking, Bethie?"

If only he wouldn't use that tone of voice when he called her "Bethie"!

"It would be too painful to tell you. Perhaps we had better go and eat."

He gently squeezed the fingers he held. "It's so good to be with you again. I'm thankful to God that He's brought us back together."

A fine mist was falling, traffic was heavy, and driving was difficult, so Clark didn't talk much as they drove to the restaurant. Later, while they waited for their meal to be served, Beth asked him, "How could seven and a half years have made such a difference? Did you think when we first knew each other that our circumstances would ever change so much? Did your dreams of the future conjure up anything like this?"

"I stopped dreaming several years ago."

Beth darted a quick look in Clark's direction, then lowered her head and nervously shifted the silverware lying in front of her. He quickly reached for her hand. "I shouldn't have said that—I don't want you to be uncomfortable."

"You couldn't make me feel any worse than I already do. I've never forgiven myself for the way I treated you on my graduation night."

"I forgave you long ago. It wasn't all your fault. I should have let you know I was coming, so it was no wonder you had made other plans—but I wanted to surprise you. I guess both of us were surprised," he added grimly. "I was late leaving the mine, and I didn't have time to change into clean clothing. I don't blame you for ignoring me."

When she didn't answer, he said, "I won't deny that some of the things that happened years ago were painful to me, and it took me a long time to be optimistic about them, but I believe that God had a hand in it. I know now it was right for you to go away to school, which you couldn't have done if you'd married me. God knew the future, and we didn't. But what occurred then needn't spoil things for us now that we're together again."

As Beth met Clark's warm gaze she knew that he truly did forgive her and believed all had worked out for the best. She wondered if he still loved her. The idea made her heart lift with joy. Then she stopped herself. Clark might have forgiven her—but she hadn't forgiven herself.

"It would be pretty low-down of me to have rejected you in the past because you couldn't offer what I wanted, and turn to you now when you've gone up a notch or two in the world," Beth replied finally. "I've treated you meanly, but I won't add insult to injury by being that kind of a person."

"I'll accept you on any terms," he said with such sincerity that Beth couldn't doubt the truth of his words.

"Surely you don't still feel the same about me as you did before I left Harlan? There must be someone else you care for, Clark." Even if Clark was too busy with his career and school to think about dating, Beth was sure many women would want to find a way to get to know him.

He shook his head. "I've taken a few women to company dinners since I've been in Lexington, but

nothing else. I told you once that I'm like my father—
we recognize the one for us when we first see her, and
no one else will do.''

Beth's pulse quickened at this declaration of his
faithfulness. ''I'm not worth that.''

''Our opinions differ.''

''I still intend to leave Harlan County as soon as I
serve my two years.''

''You might change your mind. This is one of the
best places in the world to live.''

''How would you know? You haven't lived outside
Kentucky.''

''Maybe not, but I'm proud of my heritage. This
state has one of the most colorful histories to be found
anywhere, and you'd realize that if you would forget
the dissatisfactions of your youth, or at least count the
blessings you had then. Your unhappiness was due
mostly to family problems, and that could have happened to you no matter where you lived. Why not give
Kentucky another try before you write it off?''

''I don't have any other choice, for now.''

''Will you at least keep an open mind, not stick to
some preconceived notion that you want to leave as
soon as you can?''

''I'll try. If I accomplish all of the things Mr.
Shriver expects of me, I'll be so busy that I won't have
any time to worry about the past or think of the future.''

''And as for our relationship,'' he added, ''you
know how I feel about you, but while you sort out
your feelings, may we at least be friends?''

Beth had never doubted that she loved Clark, but

life with him had never seemed to be the fulfillment of her dreams. Here was a man she could have for the taking, so why was she still hesitant? For years she had denied what her heart wanted and listened to her will. Was it time to start listening to her heart?

"I hope that I'm worthy to be your friend, Clark. You were certainly a good one when we were in high school. I probably would have quit school if you hadn't been so kind to me."

"But you had other friends."

"A few, but I've always been slow at making friends. I know lots of people, but I can count my close friends on my fingers."

"That's going to change. Things are going to look up for you, Bethie."

As they were driving back to the motel, Clark said, "You will recall, I hope, the only present I've ever given you—the Bible—as a Christmas gift once. Have you read it?"

"Yes, I have—some. But I can't say that it's had any impact on my life. I haven't found the comfort in it that you said I would," she admitted.

"I'd hoped you would draw strength from the Scriptures when you were away at school. I prayed for you every day."

"Then your prayers must have kept me going on days when I didn't think I could possibly survive. I didn't have the educational background for some of the chemistry and science courses I had to take in nursing school, and when I worked twenty hours a week for spending money, I didn't have sufficient time to study. I often took tests when I didn't think I would get one answer correct, but when I started working out the problems, I became calm, and I recalled many of the demonstrations we'd had in class. Your prayers must have worked the miracle.'' The very thought was confusing to Beth, and she looked at Clark in amazement.

"I'd like to think so,'' he said gently.

When Beth had read the Bible, she had done so to get a sense of Clark's presence, but she wasn't about to tell him that. She didn't want to give him any false hope. "I mainly read the Scriptures you had underlined. One I committed to memory was, 'Whatsoever thy hand findeth to do, do *it* with thy might.'''

"That's a good one to remember.''

Beth nodded. "It more or less became my motto. I was determined that I was going to earn my degree, although it was difficult.''

"We have to work for anything we want badly enough. Fortunately, the most important thing in life is free, and we don't have to lift a hand to get it.''

Beth turned questioning green eyes in his direction.

"I'm talking about God's gift of eternal life. We have that because Jesus died on the cross to save all mankind—there's nothing we can do to earn it.''

Beth nodded. She didn't understand what he meant, but right now she didn't want to discuss the subject.

When they arrived at the motel, Clark walked into the lobby with her. "Do you want me to stop by for you in the morning?''

"No, I can find my way to Shriver headquarters. What time should we be there?''

"Nine o'clock will be all right.''

"I should be in a better frame of mind to discuss my job description in the morning. I fear Mr. Shriver formed a poor opinion of me this morning."

"Don't worry about it. He'll be kind to you, no matter what he thought."

Clark was waiting in his vehicle when Beth pulled into the Shriver parking lot the next morning, and she stopped her car beside his. By the time she had turned off the engine and picked up her purse, he was opening the car door.

"Good morning," he said. "You look rested. Did you sleep well?"

Falling into step beside him as they walked toward the office building, she said brightly, "As a matter of fact, I did. I've been dreading coming back to Kentucky, but I feel as if I've gotten over the worst hurdle—"

"Meeting me?" he interrupted, and although he spoke lightly, she surmised that he feared what she might say.

"Don't put words in my mouth," she said. "I mean, I'm amazed that I actually had the nerve to come back at all when I dreaded it so much. You were included in that, but you're not the only reason." He opened the door for her and waved to the receptionist.

"I didn't suppose I'd even see you, and certainly not on my first day here," Beth continued. "I wasn't looking forward to meeting you after I'd treated you so shabbily. I was so busy at school that I didn't often have time to think, but when the time came for me to return, I started fretting about coming home. Last night I accepted what's before me, and I feel relieved.''

"Then you've buried the past?''

"I didn't say that. I simply mean that I've decided to continue my school motto into the new job. 'Whatsoever thy hand findeth to do, do it with thy might.' I'm going to give this two-year stint with Shriver Mining Company the best I have, and let the future take care of itself.''

The door to Milton Shriver's office was open and they walked in. Shriver was talking on the phone, and Clark motioned Beth toward the connecting office.

"You might as well see my bailiwick, while we wait for him to finish that call,'' he said. "I think being the boss's nephew had some bearing on getting this office, or perhaps Milton just wants to keep his eye on me.''

Beth glanced around the spacious room, which was brightened by the morning sun streaming in the picture window that overlooked a small garden area. Modern, walnut office furniture was clustered conveniently around a conference table, and a computer station was located beside Clark's desk.

"Well, this is an improvement over the tree stand,'' she said, and try as she might, she couldn't stop her lower lip from quivering.

"So you haven't forgotten that!'' Taking her arm, he guided her toward a maroon leather chair. When she was seated, he perched on the side of his desk. "It's still there,'' he said. "I climb the mountain sometimes when I go home to visit my parents.''

Milton Shriver appeared in the doorway. "I'm free

for a few minutes, and I've instructed Stephanie to hold my calls. Come in.'' He looked at Beth keenly. "Feeling all right now?"

"Yes, sir, and ready to start working."

"You must sit in on our meeting, Clark. You will be in closer contact with Miss Warner than I. I don't suppose you'll find that tedious."

Clark colored slightly. "I believe I'll be able to handle it."

Beth lowered her eyes to avoid the humorous look on Shriver's face. Had Clark told him something about them, or had Shriver only detected an undercurrent in their relationship after her embarrassing behavior yesterday?

Shriver shuffled through some papers on his desk and handed Beth a file folder.

"You'll find our plans for the clinic in this folder. This is what we propose, Miss Warner. I would suggest that you go to Harlan County, see where we intend to establish the clinic, and spend a month canvasing the county to assess what type of program you believe will be the most helpful to our employees there—both the retired miners, and those presently working. Our office staff can provide you with a list of Shriver workers in that area. Are you well-acquainted with the county roads?"

"No, except for the small district where we lived. In the last years of his life, my father was hardly able to leave Warner Hollow, except when he went to the doctor, and Mom and I didn't have an opportunity to go anywhere, either."

"Then, Clark, you had better plan to spend several weeks in Harlan County to help Miss Warner."

Several weeks with Clark. Beth's mind reeled at the prospect. To hide her reaction she glanced down at the papers, and felt overwhelmed at the scope of what was expected of her. "At the end of a month, I hope you can propose a schedule to implement our plans," Shriver continued. "Is that asking too much?"

"Probably," Beth answered, with a chuckle. "But I'll never know until I'm in the field."

"Of course, you can ask for an extension of time, if necessary."

She slowly shook her head. "No, I'll have something for you to consider within a month."

"Clark," Shriver said, "you see that Miss Warner has a computer and any other equipment she might need in taking this survey." Turning to Beth again, he asked, "Any questions?"

"I'll have to arrange for a place to live. Do you know if there are any apartments available for rent in Harlan?"

"There's a small apartment available for your use at the clinic," Shriver explained. "After a while you may want to find something else, but that should be adequate for a month."

"I'm opposed to her staying there at night," Clark interjected. "It's too isolated."

"She'll have a telephone, and it's only ten miles into town." Shriver turned to Beth. "We've discussed this before and can't seem to agree. Will you be afraid to stay alone? The nearest neighbor is a mile away."

"I don't think so," Beth said slowly. "I'll just have to find out by experience."

"Then there isn't anything to be gained by delay. You can leave for eastern Kentucky whenever you like."

"Yes, I'm eager to start." Beth looked toward Clark. "I assume that you'll need to show me where I'll be working."

"Yes, of course, but since I may be away from the office for several weeks, I have some work to complete today. I can arrange to leave in the morning."

"I want to visit my friend, Pam, and I learned that she's moved back to Pineville. I phoned her last night, so I'll go as far as her home today and meet you in front of the courthouse in Harlan tomorrow."

They agreed to meet at noon the next day, and Beth left the building and drove to the motel to get her belongings. With some misgivings, but also with anticipation, she drove south on I-75. She had telephoned Pam, who insisted that Beth should spend the night with them. Her delight in a reunion seemed genuine, and Beth was eager to see her friend again.

The extensive, fertile farms along the interstate, and the large black barns were distinctive of this part of Kentucky. Sleek horses and purebred cattle roamed the meadows. Spacious homes were surrounded by well-manicured lawns, and even in the bleak winter weather, the area was beautiful. To the east lay the Cumberland Mountains, while westward, broad level fields could be seen. Kentucky was indeed a land of contrasts.

There was the usual grouping of restaurants, motels,

and commercial buildings around the highway where Beth left the interstate. But after she'd driven southeast for a few miles, the landscape became more rugged and undeveloped.

When she arrived at Pineville, Beth saw the flood-wall and was reminded of how often eastern Kentucky had been ravaged by floods until such engineering projects brought relief. Situated in the flood plain of the Cumberland River, this small town had been del-uged repeatedly by spring floods until the erection of the high wall that now protected it. Floods were still a threat to the rural areas and small towns without floodwalls, and almost every spring, some area of the state was devastated by high water.

Beth had no trouble following Pam's directions to her home, and when she parked in the driveway, Pam rushed out to envelop her in a hug, and Beth's throat tightened as she clung to her friend. With an arm around Beth's shoulders, Pam guided her into the house.

"I'm home alone at the present," she said. "Grace, our four-year-old, is at kindergarten. We'll pick her up in a couple of hours, but that will be long enough for us to talk over old times." She put both hands on Beth's shoulders and held her at arm's length.

"Let's see if you've changed." After close scrutiny, Pam said, "Still pretty as a picture, but not very happy if I'm any judge." She dropped her hands. "Come in the kitchen, and we'll have a cup of coffee."

"No coffee, please," Beth replied, "but I would like a glass of ice water."

While Pam took ice from the refrigerator and filled

her glass, Beth scanned the small room, which was bright and cheerful with white cabinets, yellow curtains, and shining appliances. No doubt about it, Pam was a born housewife. She hadn't changed a great deal, but she was thinner than she had been. Her blond hair flowed freely over her shoulders, and her brown eyes glistened with excitement.

"I've thought about you so much, Beth, and wondered what was happening to you. How are matters between you and Alex Connor?"

Beth shook her head. "I haven't heard anything from him since he left Prestonburg."

"And is that the cause of your unhappiness?"

"Very little of it. I was flattered to have a sophisticated man like Alex take an interest in me, but I'm ashamed to admit that I was awed by the idea of the things Alex could provide that I'd never had," Beth admitted. "At first, I was humiliated because he could forget me so easily, but I didn't love him. I've not tried to contact him."

"So how does it feel to be back in Kentucky?"

Beth shrugged. "I had to come back to fulfill the promise I made when I took the scholarship from Shriver Mining."

"But you didn't want to come, and that has made you unhappy," Pam stated as she settled into a chair opposite Beth and passed her a plate of cookies.

Beth munched on a chocolate cookie before she answered. "Perhaps. There are many things here that I want to forget."

Pam toyed with the cup in front of her, and without

looking at Beth, she said softly, "Clark Randolph, for instance?"

Beth's face flushed. "I knew it wasn't likely that I could avoid seeing Clark during the two years I'm obligated to live in this area, but I certainly didn't expect him to be my boss. As far as I knew, he was still digging coal in Harlan County, and when I met him as an executive at Shriver's corporate offices yesterday, I was stunned."

"You had no idea?"

Beth shook her head.

"And he's really going to be your boss?" Pam asked, a smile creasing her face.

"I'm to be in charge of a new health clinic sponsored by the mining company, and Clark will be my liaison with the company. He's to help me set up the system, and I'll be responsible to him."

"When are you going to admit that you love Clark Randolph, marry him, and make both of you happy?"

"I gave up any right to Clark several years ago, so there's no use talking about it."

"I'm going to tell you something, Beth, that I should have told you long ago. That night you graduated and, from your own account, shunned Clark and went off with Alex, he came to our house, and I've never seen a man so low. Except for Clark's strong spiritual convictions, I think he would have taken his own life. He told us how he'd loved you for years, and how you had turned him down."

"Oh, don't, Pam," Beth cried. "I know I hurt him, but I can't stand to hear about it."

"Ray advised him to forget you," Pam continued

relentlessly. "Told him you weren't worth the trouble you'd caused him."

Beth winced at that, but Pam talked on. "Clark said he had no choice—that you'd become a part of his life the first time he saw you, and there was no way he could remove you from his heart."

Beth closed her ears with her fingers and would listen to no more. When Pam stopped talking, Beth said, "I came here for some comfort, not a lecture. I'm already hurting enough. I'm sorry for the way I treated Clark, but it's done, and I can't change it."

"I won't say anything more," Pam said, throwing up her hands. "But at least, I hope you've learned your lesson. The woman who marries Clark Randolph will be very fortunate indeed."

Beth took a large swallow of the water she had asked for and stood. "I'll be leaving now, Pam."

"Leaving! I thought you were going to stay all night."

"I thought so, too, but I have the feeling I'm not welcome."

"All right, I'll behave," Pam said with a laugh. "Not another word about Clark. You do know you're welcome here." She put her arms around Beth and hugged her tightly, and Beth clung to her.

"Sorry to be so edgy, but Clark is a touchy subject with me," she said, and sitting down again, she stared out the window to the backyard where playground equipment was set up. "I dread to go back to Harlan County, and I want you to give me some of your down-to-earth advice."

"Let's take a walk around town," Pam suggested,

as she reached for a coat hanging on the kitchen door. "It's a nice day, and I haven't been out of the house."

"Good. I need some exercise, too. I've been driving for a few days."

Beth shrugged into her jacket, and they started down the street.

"Why do you dread to go back to your native county?"

"First of all, I suppose I don't want to run into my brothers and sister. My brothers were such crude people, and Luellen, my sister, really made life miserable for me as a child. None of them ever liked me, as you know."

"That isn't hard to figure out. They were jealous of you, and of your mother, because their father loved both of you."

"I remember one time, though, when Luellen wanted me around. She was visiting at our home on Christmas Day when she went into labor with her youngest son. A snowstorm had closed the road up the mountain, and she couldn't get home, so they sent me to bring Granny Warner. Let me tell you, that night was an experience for me."

"Really opened your eyes to what womanhood is, huh?" Pam said, laughing.

"I'll say. At first, I was appalled by her suffering, but then I began to see what a bond there was between a mother and her child. Granny made me sit beside Luellen and hold her hands, and when the pains were severe, she would grip my hand and mutter. 'Don't leave me, Beth. I can't stand to be alone, and Joe won't come. He doesn't love me. Where is Joe? I want him with me.'"

"A woman isn't always conscious of what she's saying during labor."

"Whatever she meant by her ramblings, Luellen was glad to have me with her that night, but that's the only time I've ever felt close to her."

"Well, I wouldn't worry about it, for you probably won't see much of your family. I've heard that your brothers got into some kind of trouble and left the area for good. So what else is bothering you?"

"When I show up as the company's nurse, will everyone still see me as 'that poor Warner girl,' and not want to put their health in my hands?"

"To the contrary, they might think you'll be just like Granny Warner and flock to you for help." Pam tucked her hand under Beth's arm. "All of your life you've been running away from something—from your home life, your siblings, your hardships. And from Clark," she added softly. "It's time you stood your ground and started to live."

"That's what I intended to do, but not in Harlan County. I know you think I'm being foolish, but you've always had a calm, well-adjusted life."

Pam laughed in her quiet, unhurried way. "My life hasn't been without its problems. You remember how my parents opposed my marriage to Ray, and how it took them a long time to forgive me. And, of course, financially we've often had problems. Ray's income as a musician is irregular. 'Feast today, famine tomorrow' has characterized our finances. But we've been happy and are still in love. That's the kind of marriage I want for you, so forgive me for meddling in your affairs.''

Beth nodded, but she couldn't answer.

Chapter Four

Beth arrived in Harlan two hours before she had to meet Clark, so she parked her car in front of the court-house and set out to explore the town. Since the sun was shining, she put on dark glasses, hoping to avoid anyone who might recognize her, for she wasn't ready to renew past acquaintances.

She passed the library where she had often gone for books. Soon she came to the school complex, noting a sign touting the school's champion basketball team—the Green Dragons. At the elementary school nearby, children were out for recess, enjoying them-selves on the playground equipment. One girl stood alone, a pensive expression on her face, looking as if she wanted to be a part of the merriment, but hesitat-ing, perhaps from fear of rejection.

The child reminded Beth of her own behavior the first month she had attended school in Harlan. It had been a miserable experience, but fortunately she had soon made friends, and the year at Harlan High School may well have been the happiest period of her life.

Harlan was located in a narrow valley of Martins Fork of the Cumberland River, and from the crowded downtown section, houses stretched up the mountainside. She passed the house where she had lived with her grandmother, but it needed paint and the porch roof sagged, and she wished she hadn't seen it.

She paused in front of a small church that reminded her of the one she had attended when she lived with her grandmother. Grandma Ella hadn't made many rules, but when she had taken Beth after the death of John and Mary Warner, she had said to her granddaughter, "Now that you'll be living with me all the time, I expect you to go to church with me. I hope we won't have any argument about that."

And Beth hadn't argued. She was grateful to her grandmother for giving her a home, and she'd made up her mind not to contrary her in any way. Beth had listened intently to the messages of the minister and her Sunday-school teacher, searching for the faith that Clark had shown, but she had never found it.

On impulse, Beth walked up the steps of the church and tried the door, which opened to her touch, and she stepped inside.

The interior was cold and empty—as empty as her life. Years ago, she'd thought that a college education would fill the void, but she still felt incomplete. Sunlight, gleaming through the stained-glass window behind the pulpit, backlighted the small cross above the altar, and Beth eased down in the rear pew.

She was seeking something, but she didn't know

what. If it was love she lacked, Clark was ready and waiting to give himself to her. A Bible lay on the seat beside her—she reached for it and opened it.

According to Clark, it was here that the antidote for her discontent could be found. She leafed through the Bible, searching, praying that God would reveal himself to her. She had tried to pray many times, but she'd never been sure that God heard her prayers. Today, He must have, for some words on one of the pages leaped out at her.

"I am come that they might have life, and that they might have it more abundantly."

She'd been yearning for an abundant life for as long as she could remember. According to these words, Christ was the answer; that without Him, there could be no bountiful life. Somewhere in the past, she'd heard a song, and a few of the lyrics now popped into her mind. Beth sang softly, "'Without Him I would be drifting like a ship without a sail.'"

Poised as she was on the threshold of a new career, Beth remembered again her childhood dream of becoming a great person by being a blessing to other people. Because of her rebellious nature, had God punished her by sending her back to Harlan County when she so desperately wanted to start a life elsewhere? Or had He presented her with an opportunity to serve here, just as Florence Nightingale had been a comfort to soldiers on the sordid battlefields of the Crimea? Only time would tell, but when she left the church and walked toward her appointment with Clark, Beth's outlook was more optimistic than it had been for a long time.

* * *

Beth sat in the car and waited for Clark, watching the passersby, wondering if she would see anyone she knew, but his vehicle soon pulled into the parking space beside her. Remembering what Pam had told her, she felt even more diffident in his presence, but his sunny smile cheered her, and she determined to try and ignore the unpleasant incidents that had occurred between them in the past. He lowered the window and leaned toward her.

"Why not leave your car here, and we can go in the company vehicle to the clinic? After you see that, we will make further plans."

When she nodded, he jumped from the vehicle, and was on hand to open the passenger door and help her climb inside.

"Did you have a good visit with Pam and Ray?" he asked as he backed out into the narrow street and headed out of town.

"Yes, I did. It didn't take long before it felt like old times. We had a great time catching up."

"I don't see Ray much anymore. His band has gotten popular, and they're on the road a great deal. They have become good musicians. I'd like to take you to hear them sometime when they're playing in this area."

"That sounds fine," she said. At one time, Beth had thought she'd never want to hear bluegrass music again, but she believed she would enjoy it now.

When they passed the secondary road where Clark had taken her the night of his senior prom—the time he had asked her to marry him—Beth felt herself blush, and her hands clenched in her lap. She turned her face away from Clark. Well enough for her to determine to forget the past when everywhere she looked, a reminder popped up.

Clark didn't ignore her discomfiture, but laid a tender hand on her shoulder. "I, too, remember every time I drive by here. I owe you an apology for that night. I was pushing too fast—I know that now—but at eighteen, I still had a lot to learn. It was just that I loved you so much, Bethie, that I didn't want to be separated from you."

Beth couldn't answer him, but her thoughts rioted. What would her life be like now if she had said yes to Clark's proposal?

They drove in silence for a few more miles until they'd climbed a small hill, where Clark stopped in front of a one-story brick building that was surrounded by a newly paved parking lot. Scraggly evergreen shrubbery edged the foundation of the structure.

"This isn't a new building," Clark said. "It was originally built as a residence, but the company got a good deal on it and liked it particularly because it's out of the flood plain. There's a pretty view because the land slopes down to the river, but it's safe from high water."

"I suppose that would need to be considered in this area."

"There's already been some remodeling to make it into a clinic, but we'll need your professional input to fit it to your specific needs." He turned off the engine and stepped from the car. "Come on in and look it over. I came out earlier and turned up the thermostat, so it should be warm enough now.''

The front door opened into a small room that led into a larger area, undoubtedly used as the living room when the building was a residence. The rooms were bare of furniture.

"We thought this small room could be the waiting room, and we'd use the room next door for examining and treating patients," Clark explained. "We haven't bought any equipment, since that decision should be made by you and Dr. Andrews. I know it seems small, but it will take you some time to build up your practice."

Beth looked around the room. "There are plenty of possibilities here, and cabinets would have to be brought in to store medical supplies."

Clark opened a door into a large bedroom, with an adjacent bathroom. "This area can be used for storage, and the rest of the house will be your living quarters." He motioned to the large oval tub in the bathroom. "Would you want this tub removed? You might need the space more for something else."

"Oh, no, that tub is wonderful," Beth said, delighted. "If I assist at a delivery here in the clinic, that tub will be great for a water birth."

He looked confused. "I'm afraid you've lost me, there. Shows you that I don't know much about midwifery."

They entered a cozy kitchen with a dining area, and to the right of this was a large room, where a picture window provided a view of the large grassy field that led down to the river. What had probably been used as a family room, when the building was a residence, had been made into a combination living room and bedroom, with a latticed partition separating the two areas. The bedroom was furnished with a queen-size bed, a matching dresser and chest, and it opened into another bathroom. The living area had a large couch, coordinated chairs, and plenty of tables and lamps.

"Will this be convenient for you?" Clark asked anxiously.

Beth laughed. "Why wouldn't it be?" Perhaps Clark was being polite, but he knew as well as she did that the apartment was better than anything she'd ever lived in. She walked to the window and wrote her name in the condensation generated by the heat on the cold glass. "I'm not concerned about where I live, but I'm overwhelmed to think that within a month, I'm required to establish a health clinic and be ready to start seeing patients. I'm afraid."

Clark came and stood beside her. He wrote his name above hers on the steamy window with the word *loves* separating the two names, which he outlined with a heart, bisecting the heart with an arrow, similar to the one he had once carved in the bark of a beech tree on Randolph Mountain.

"Aw, Bethie, don't worry—I'll help you."

He put his arm around her shoulders, and for a moment she leaned against him, trying to gain courage from the strength and warmth of his muscular frame. He lowered his head until it touched hers, and his lips softly caressed her hair. A sense of well-being penetrated Beth's heart, but after a moment she forced herself to walk away from him, and a long sigh escaped his lips.

"What would you suggest I do first?" she asked.

"Dr. Andrews will meet us here at three o'clock this afternoon. In the meantime, do you want to move in?"

Wandering into the kitchen, Beth opened the doors of the empty cabinets. "I'll need to buy groceries, too."

"The company will advance you a month's wages, if you need it."

"No, I have enough money to manage until I've earned the wages. It won't take long to move in my possessions. I don't have much—just my clothing and books."

"I still don't like having you live here. Won't you be afraid?"

"I don't know. I shouldn't be—there's a security light, I notice, and I'll have a telephone."

"But you might have patients coming at night if there are emergencies, and that could be anyone."

Beth shrugged her shoulders. "I can't help it— that's part of the job I'll be paid to do. I'll manage."

But Beth knew he was still concerned, although he avoided further comment as they drove back into town. After lunch, she followed him back to the clinic in her car, and while Clark carried her boxes into the house, she went to a nearby grocery store and bought some basic foods for breakfast and lunch. It didn't take long for her to unpack her books and place them on the shelves in the living room, or to hang her relatively few garments in the closet area. When she finished,

Clark took the empty cartons and stored them in a small metal barn behind the house.

"I'll take you out to dinner for the first week or so," Clark told her. "Company orders," he added with a grin to forestall any objections on her part.

Dr. Andrews was middle-aged, slightly stooped, with brown eyes and graying brown hair, exhibiting a brusque manner that at first intimidated Beth; but she soon saw that behind the gruff demeanor was a warm, caring personality—a man whose life was devoted to his patients.

"Well, young lady," were his first words, "you've certainly chosen a poor profession. Ministering to the sick anyplace is bad enough, but to come to a rural region where we have more than our share of medical problems wasn't a smart move."

With a smile, to take the sting out of her words, she commented, "Then why are you practicing here?"

He waved his hand in frustration. "I'm a man with a mission—came here directly out of medical school, believing I could cure all the ills of society in a few years. I *chose* to come here, mind you! Almost twenty years later, I can't see that I've made any impact at all." He shook his head. "You should have gotten a job in a city hospital where you could have worked regular hours." He waved his big beefy hand toward the door. "Here, you'll be called out to assist in a birth, or there will be someone pounding on that door all hours of the night. You shouldn't be living here beside the clinic." He frowned at Clark.

"My opinion, exactly, so don't blame me. My superiors don't agree with me. This clinic is supposed to be a service to the people, and they contend that it won't serve its purpose if the nurse isn't on call.''

"Doctor, if it will relieve your mind—I didn't envision myself as a country nurse, either. I wanted to work in a city, but I owe Shriver Mining two years of service for the scholarship they gave me, and so I trained in a field that would do the most good here. I can't say that I consider this is my mission in life, but I've accepted this job, and while I'm here, I'm going to give it the best that's in me. After that, there are facilities springing up all over the country where my skills are needed, and I can probably take my pick.''

Dr. Andrews reached for her hand and squeezed it. "Then you and I will get along all right. And if it's any relief to you, I don't get much sleep either, so if you have a midnight patient, I'm as near as the telephone.'' He stood and surveyed the room. "Let's go to work.''

It took a week for Beth to come up with what she considered an adequate working plan for the clinic. Dr. Andrews had provided her with stacks of catalogs to order supplies and equipment. As she listed the things she would need, she drew up a floor plan to show where each item would be placed. Dr. Andrews stopped by every afternoon, and approved or disapproved her plans. He particularly helped her with the medicines she should order.

"You won't have to stock many drugs here—you can write prescriptions and they can order them at a pharmacy. We can confer on any major ailment, and if you don't feel you can handle it, we'll take the patient to the hospital. Of course, you'll have the equipment to do some diagnostic testing, but just understand that we're working as a team. The clinic and the hospital aren't competing—we are here to meet the health needs of our patients.''

''I've ordered several home birth kits for parents to keep at home. I've also put several fetoscopes and ultrasonic stethoscopes on my list of necessities. Besides oxygen tanks in case of an emergency, I'll need drugs that can slow or stop a hemorrhage.''

''Beth, I'll work along with you on these home births. Why don't you arrange to have me examine the women a couple of times? That will corroborate your opinion and probably make you more comfortable.''

''I'd appreciate it, and if complications should arise, you'd be familiar with the case. I've helped with a lot of births, but I've never been completely on my own. Of course, in the case of a high-risk pregnancy, I will refer the patient to you from the start.''

When the preliminary plan was finished, Dr. Andrews faxed a copy to Milton Shriver, and a day later, he gave them his official okay in a fax:

Well pleased with what you have done. Order any materials you need, hire any necessary workmen, and be ready to open the doors in three weeks.

While they waited for the hospital equipment to be shipped, Clark hired workmen to come in to transform the former living quarters into a clinic. New water lines, drainage, and electrical outlets were installed, and dressing rooms partitioned. Carpet was installed in the waiting room and new floor tile laid in the examination area.

After a week of exhaustive labor, on Saturday afternoon, Clark said, "Mother would like for you to come to our home for supper this evening."

Beth knew that Clark stayed with his parents when he was in this area, and she had been curious about his family.

"Oh, I don't know, Clark." She lifted a hand to her hair. "I look pretty tacky—it's been a hard week."

"All the more reason you should be treated to one of my mother's meals. You've been existing on yogurt, peanut butter, and crackers all week."

"Doesn't sound very healthy for a nurse, does it?" she admitted. "But I have eaten lots of fruit and raw vegetables, too."

When she still hesitated, he took her hand. "Please, Bethie. It would mean a great deal to me to have you meet my family. I have to be back in Lexington on Monday morning, so I'll be gone for several days."

Without meeting his eyes, she said, "Okay, I'll go. What time?"

"I have to go into town, but I'll pick you up about four o'clock. That will give you time to rest a bit."

Beth filled the tub with hot water, poured in some bubble bath and soaked her tired body. When the water cooled, she added more hot water. While she luxuriated in the soothing bath, with eyes closed, she contemplated her relationship with Clark. *What was she going to do about him?*

If he wasn't concerned about her previous rejection

of him, why should she be? She didn't excuse herself for not realizing his true worth, but Clark seemed to understand that she had been too young to make the decisions he'd demanded of her.

She supposed that if she was wise, she would just throw her concerns to the wind, forget about the future and marry Clark. His devotion to her was so obvious that it was sometimes embarrassing. While she didn't believe Clark Randolph would be a doormat for anyone, he did remind her of a faithful pet that owed loyalty to only one master. No woman could ask for more in a man.

But two other matters caused her to hesitate. She still had no desire to spend her life in a rural area, and she knew that, in spite of his employment in Lexington, Clark's heart was in the mountains of eastern Kentucky and always would be.

But the most difficult hurdle was Clark's Christian faith and her lack of it. How did one grow in the faith? She believed in God, so why didn't she have that personal walk with Him that she had observed in Clark and her grandmother? She determined that she would start a daily routine of meditation—read the Bible, try to pray. *Should she enlist Clark to pray on her behalf?*

Drying herself as the water drained from the tub, Beth asked a question that she knew she must answer. *Did she love Clark enough to stay here forever?* She had lain awake every night since she had returned to Kentucky, trying to know her heart. And the last couple of weeks when she had been so much in his presence, she knew that she did love him very much. How could she not love a man like Clark? He possessed every quality she admired and respected. And beyond that, from the very first, she had felt something special each time she so much as looked at him—attraction, longing, tenderness. Feelings she'd never had for anyone but Clark.

She believed that Clark would make any sacrifice for her happiness, short of denying his commitment to the Lord Jesus and leaving Kentucky, and she actually believed she could persuade him to move away. But there was no doubt in her mind where Clark's first loyalty lay—he wouldn't deny his Lord even for her. Did she love him enough to give up her own goals to join him in this area that would always be his home, no matter where he lived? Before many months, she would have to make that decision.

Beth's wardrobe was so limited that it didn't take long to choose a pair of brown plaid wool slacks and a green turtleneck sweater to wear to dinner. When she received her first paycheck, perhaps she would splurge on some new clothes. She had ordered several nurse's outfits, so she had no more money for clothing now, but even dressed in old garments, she didn't find her image in the mirror displeasing and she hoped to make a good impression on Clark's family.

"These forests were always bleak in the winter," Beth commented as they drove along the road that the Warners had traveled on their sporadic trips into Harlan.

"But they're still beautiful," Clark said. "This time of year, you can see the configuration of the earth. Those rock outcroppings could have come from a sculptor's hand, and look at the gnarled oak trunks and branches. The hills are beautiful when the trees are in leaf, but I like them all the time."

"Is there anything about Kentucky that you don't like?" she teased, but, of course, he was right, Beth thought, as she looked at the forest through his eyes. Did she need Clark at her side to be able to see the beauty that life offered?

"What do your folks know about us?" she asked.

He gave her a quick look. "Nothing to make you uncomfortable. They know that you used to live in Harlan County, but I've never told them anything about my personal interest in you."

"You won't have to tell them," Beth said with a light laugh. "If you look at me the way you do most of the time, it won't take long for your parents to know. They may not be pleased."

"Surely you aren't thinking about that Warner-Randolph feud?"

Beth shook her head. "I'm referring to my lack of faith." She met his eyes steadily as he glanced her way. "But I want to believe as you do, Clark. I really do. I've decided to schedule a daily time to read the Bible and try to pray. Will you pray for me, too?"

Guiding the vehicle with one hand, he covered her nervous fingers with his warm right hand. "Why, Bethie, I told you that I've been praying for you every day for years—not only that you will accept the Truth, but that you will agree to be my wife."

"Looks like you should have given up praying by now, since God hasn't answered."

"Oh, He's answered, all right, but He said to 'be

patient.' I've tried to be, and someday I'm going to have what I want." He released her hand. "But about praying—your path to God is through his Son, Jesus. Until you accept Jesus as your Savior, God won't hear any of your prayers, except when you say, 'God, be merciful to me, a sinner.'"

Beth shook her head and looked out the window. "This is so confusing. It's as if you're on a different wavelength than mine."

Clark left the highway, drove a short distance up a narrow hollow and stopped before a one-story brick house, located beside a small stream.

"When the girls started going to the consolidated high school, Daddy rented that little house in Harlan, and they live here all of the time. After I started working for the company, I had the solid-brick veneer put on, but it's the same house we lived in when I was a boy."

The door opened and a man, supported by a cane, walked out onto the porch and lifted a hand.

"My daddy," Clark said, and pride was evident in his voice. "Talk to him about your spiritual doubts," Clark whispered in her ear. "Remember, he's a preacher."

"Beth, this is my daddy, Abner Randolph. And this is Beth."

Mr. Randolph shook her hand and motioned Beth into a small, but immaculate, living room. A tall woman stood beside a table, looking at Beth with intent brown eyes just like her son's. *So Clark was a Shriver rather than a Randolph. No wonder Milton Shriver had taken such an interest in him.* She had noticed that Milton and Clark had several family traits in common, but the resemblance was more marked between Anna Randolph and her son.

"Mother, I want you to meet Beth Warner." Beth had never heard Clark's voice more vibrant and warm than when he introduced her to his mother. It was obvious that bringing the woman he loved together with his parents, whom he equally loved and honored, was one of the greatest moments of his life. Who wouldn't love a man like that?

"You're welcome to our home, Beth. We're happy that the clinic is opening and that you are the one to head it," Anna said. "I'm sorry that we didn't know you when you lived here before, but after Abner was injured, we didn't circulate a lot."

With a chuckle, Mr. Randolph said, "This is the first time we've ever had a Warner under our roof, Beth. Suppose it might cause another family feud?"

With a slight laugh, Beth replied, "I don't think so. I'm not the feuding kind."

"Neither are we, but I have had your brothers cross the street rather than meet me."

"Daddy! You shouldn't tease Beth about something she can't help."

"Forgive me, Beth, and I was only teasing."

"I'm not much like my brothers and sister, for we didn't have the same mother. I don't share any of their prejudices."

"Enough of that," Mrs. Randolph told them. "The three of you sit and visit while I finish up supper." When Beth made a move to assist her, she said, "I have everything well under way—you rest for a while. Clark says you've been mighty busy this week.''

And it was good to ease down in a soft chair and listen while Clark and his father chatted about the day's events.

When Anna announced that the meal was ready, she said, "I'm sorry you won't meet our two girls. They both have Saturday jobs, and they had already made plans for the evening before we knew you were coming.''

Beth hoped she could hide her relief at that news. Meeting all of Clark's family at one time might have proved daunting.

The house had no dining room, so they gathered around the large oval table in the kitchen. Beth didn't realize how hungry she was until Mrs. Randolph set a tray of hot homemade rolls beside her—their aroma tantalized her taste buds. The baked ham, sweet-potato casserole, green beans and coleslaw were delicious, and when she took additional servings, Beth said, "Mrs. Randolph, I'm not usually so greedy, but I haven't had a meal like this since I last sat at my grandmother's table.''

"Eat all you like, Beth. Don't you know how to cook?''

"My mother and grandmother gave me plenty of lessons in cooking, but when I was in college I ate most of my meals in the school cafeteria. I had no opportunity to cook, but now that I'm in my own apartment, I'm going to start. After I've practiced a little, I'll ask you to try one of my meals.''

"We'll like that.'' Anna replied with a warm smile.

* * *

Beth helped remove the dishes from the table and dried them after Anna scrubbed them in soapy water and rinsed them well. The older woman had a way of putting Beth at ease, and she was quite relaxed when Clark's mother surprised her by asking, "So how long has my son been in love with you?"

After a few startled moments, Beth smiled and said, "You'll have to ask him." Then, with a little chuckle, she added, "I knew it wouldn't take you long to learn his secret."

"I half expected it already. Since he's been working with you, seeing you every day, he's been happier than I've ever seen him. His voice is different, almost reverent, when he talks about you. And you're the first girl he's ever brought home for us to meet. I was sure his interest in you was more than a professional one, but he surely didn't develop such devotion in the past few weeks."

"We've been friends since we were in high school, but we couldn't have an open friendship because my father was anti-Randolph." Beth dried a cup deliberately before she added, "But I don't want you to misunderstand—we don't have plans of any kind."

"So the devotion is all on Clark's part—you don't love him?"

"I didn't say that," Beth answered ruefully. "There are some barriers between us.... I'm not the kind of person you would want for your son."

Mrs. Randolph looked at her quickly. "That's hard to believe. I don't think Clark would choose a girl that we wouldn't approve of."

"I was referring to our differences in spiritual beliefs."

"Then you aren't a Christian?"

Beth shook her head. "No, but I want to be. I've vowed to start reading the Bible, and perhaps God will reveal Himself to me."

"Anyone who calls on God with an honest and penitent heart will have no trouble finding Him. One of the ancient prophets said it well—'Then you will call upon me and come and pray to me, and I will listen to you. You will seek me and find me when you seek me with all your heart.' You see, Beth, the Scriptures tell us that it's not God's will that anyone should perish, but that all should come to repentance."

"I'm seeking, and I am hopeful that I'll find Him, but that isn't the only barrier between Clark and me. I don't want to spend the rest of my life in this area."

Anna nodded when she paused. "And, of course, Clark does."

"I didn't have a happy childhood, and my parents are both gone, so I don't have any ties to bind me here. My siblings and I have never been close. I just think I'll be happier elsewhere."

"Without Clark?"

Tears stung Beth's eyes, and she shook her head. "I don't know."

"I gave up a lot of material comforts when I married Abner, but I've lived for almost thirty years secure in his love and I've never been sorry." With a laugh, Anna added, "I tell Abner that he's just like a Canada goose—they supposedly mate for life, you know. Clark takes after his father in that respect."

To change from the subject that was painful to her, Beth said, "This is pretty china, Mrs. Randolph. It reminds me of some my mother used to have."

"It came from the Shriver Mining company store many years ago, so your mother may have had the same pattern."

Perhaps sensing Beth's discomfort, Anna followed her lead, and the rest of the evening went smoothly while the four of them visited together.

"I like your folks," Beth said, as they left the Randolph house. "I didn't realize how much I missed my own parents. It was like being home again."

"You do have some good memories, then?"

"My parents were very good to me, but you remember how my father was always sick. I realize now that I lived with the anxiety that he might die anytime. We were also poor, hardly getting by on his pension. I never went hungry, but otherwise we didn't have much. It was discouraging, even before their tragic deaths, but after that, life around here seemed impossible."

He opened his mouth as if he would remonstrate with her, but perhaps deciding this wasn't the time, Clark said nothing.

"We didn't fool your mother for long," Beth said with a grin in his direction.

"I know. I wasn't trying to hide my feelings for you. If I had your permission, I'd broadcast them to the world."

"You don't have my permission...yet."

He slanted a glance at her, but she wouldn't meet his gaze.

"What are you doing tomorrow?"

"Working," Beth said, groaning. "I still have a lot to do before we meet with Mr. Shriver next Friday."

"You need a rest. I'd hoped you would spend tomorrow with me."

"Doing what?"

"The weather is going to be warm and sunny. We could go to church in the morning, and perhaps in the afternoon, I could take you out to your old home place."

"Who owns the property now? We might not be welcome."

"Your brothers sold it to our company, so we have a legitimate right to look around."

"Do they intend to mine there?"

"No definite plans for anything now. Would it bother you if they did?"

"Probably not. I might be able to put unpleasant memories behind me if it were gone. But, yes, I will spend the day with you tomorrow. I want to go to church, and I guess I need to go to my old home—I'll keep dreading it until I do."

"I'll come for you about nine o'clock. Ours is a conservative church, so you'll be more comfortable if you wear a dress."

With a grin, Beth said, "And you and your parents will be, too?"

"My parents will, at least. You know that I'll approve of whatever you wear."

Chapter Five

Beth didn't want to be an embarrassment to Clark's parents, so she chose a calf-length dress in a floral print on a dark green background, a minimum of makeup, and a silver chain with a cross attached—a high-school graduation gift from Pam Gordon. She had rarely worn the necklace, hesitating to explain wearing a crucifix when she hadn't accepted its principles as her own.

She must have looked rather pensive when she got into the vehicle, for Clark immediately reached for her hand.

"Anything wrong?"

"A little nervous, I guess. I haven't been to church since my grandmother died."

"You'll be all right. I've warned Daddy not to single you out, although people will want to talk to you. Our members always welcome visitors, but I'll be right beside you, so don't worry about it."

The church was a new brick edifice with a sanctuary

that would hold about a hundred worshipers. A bell in the small steeple was pealing out a welcome as Clark parked in the churchyard, and children were hurrying into the Bible classes held at the back of the building.

The service was less formal than those of the church Beth had attended with Grandma Ella. The singing was boisterous and loud, and as Abner delivered the sermon in a quiet, but authoritative voice, the congregation participated by responding with, "Amen," or, "That's right," or other affirming statements.

Abner was obviously not a polished speaker, for his grammar was faulty, the diction sometimes antiquated, and the delivery unskilled, but when he quoted Scripture, there was no hesitancy in his words.

As Abner read his text for the sermon, Beth flashed a quick look in Clark's direction, and he shrugged his shoulders lightly, a smile lurking in his warm brown eyes.

Surely those words weren't in the Bible, but Abner repeated them, this time giving the chapter and the verse. "I have learned, in whatsoever state I am, therewith to be content."

Beth was unfamiliar with the verse. Still, she thought, surely that didn't mean the state of Kentucky!

But Abner's explanation was more general, saying the verse indicated that outward circumstances should not determine an individual's peace of mind or spiritual maturity. He cited examples from the Bible to prove his point.

Paul and Silas had sung praises to God during the night they spent in the Philippian jail.

In the Old Testament, Ruth, the destitute Moabitess,

was content to glean in the fields of Boaz, thankful to find enough grain for her daily food.

One verse he quoted from The Proverbs tugged at Beth's spiritual heartstrings. "The way of transgressors is hard."

Could much of the dissatisfaction with her life stem, not from outward circumstances, but from the fact that her heart wasn't right with God? She remembered the serenity of her grandmother even in times of adversity. She looked around the room, and while some of the people seemed distressed, the faces of most were peaceful and filled with hope as they fastened their eyes on Abner. One could discern by looking at these people that they hadn't had an easy time in their lives. Beth remembered hearing someone say once, "If you straighten out your own life, the rest of the world won't look so bad."

Had she wasted all of her youth pining for things she couldn't have, when she should have been satisfied with her lot in life? Had she frittered away her youth without acknowledging a need for God, when she could have enjoyed peace within by accepting His plan for her life?

Abner closed his sermon with another line of Scripture: "To be spiritually minded is life and peace."

Beth knew she had a lot to think about.

After the benediction, Clark introduced Beth to many people as "the nurse who will be opening Shriver's clinic." He also brought forward his two sisters, eighteen-old Mary Lynn, and Sallie, two years younger. The girls were friendly enough, but she suspected a hint of possessiveness—as if they weren't ready to share their adored older brother with anyone else. She couldn't much blame them. After her bad experience with her own brothers, it would be wonderful to have a brother like Clark. *But he would make a better husband.* The thought came unbidden, and it wasn't altogether welcome. In spite of the sermon she had squirmed under, she hadn't changed her mind about the place where she *didn't* want to spend the rest of her life.

Clark took her into Harlan for lunch, and then they stopped at the clinic where both of them changed into jeans and jackets, as well as heavy boots. Despite the balmy weather, the road up Randolph Mountain was as hard to navigate as it had been when Beth had come here almost a month ago. Clark shifted into four-wheel drive at the foot of the incline, and plowed slowly but steadily through the deep mud toward the summit. He took his eyes from the road briefly to flash Beth a grin.

"I don't know how you ever made it up this hill in your car."

"I don't, either," Beth admitted. "And I'm not even a good driver—I haven't had much experience."

When they reached the ridge, Clark paused and they silently surveyed the narrow hollow surrounded by steep hills, the ramshackle deserted buildings, and the curving muddy roadway over which they must travel to get there.

"Now, honestly, Clark, seeing where I spent the first sixteen years of my life, can't you understand why I didn't want the rest of my life to be like that?" She made a weary gesture toward the place that had been her home.

"It didn't have to be that way. I would have provided you something better."

"But we didn't know that seven years ago. If I had married a coal miner, I could very well have ended up in another home like this one."

"All right," he said with anger—an emotion she hadn't seen him display before. "I've admitted that I was in the wrong to press you to marry me. Just forget the past."

They sat in silence for a few moments, each lost in their own thoughts. Beth wanted badly to say something conciliatory, but feared how Clark would react to anything she said now.

Finally, she spoke. "I realize now that life is more than material possessions, because I'm no happier now than I was when I didn't have anything, but the past is still there."

Seemingly ashamed of his burst of anger, Clark said quietly, "Everyone has a past that shapes their present and future, for good or bad, and today should be a turning point for you. The fact that you were willing to come home is a large step forward."

He released the brake and gently followed the slope into the hollow. Beth clenched her hands and the knuckles had whitened by the time Clark parked in front of the house. It was depressing to see that the porch railing had collapsed. Clark turned off the ignition, but he didn't speak.

Beth closed her eyes to blot out the memories that flooded her mind. She could see her parents sitting on the porch in the late-summer evening, when the lightning bugs were illuminating the hollow with their twinkling, and the whippoorwills had started their repetitious warbling that sometimes lasted all night. Beth remembered that she'd been content then.

But there had been other times when her brothers were visiting, haranguing their father to finance one of their shady ventures, and Beth had been frightened. Even after her mother had hustled her to bed, Beth could still hear their arguments. Perhaps they had wanted to involve her father in their scheme and he had refused, for he was a moral man and would never do anything illegal, even to improve his financial state.

Her worst memory was of the moment when she had realized that her mother was dead, and then had run to the porch only to see her father slump to the floor, gasping for his last breath.

Beth opened her eyes, and breathing a deep sigh, she said, "We might as well go in."

"You want me to go with you?"

"Please. I can't face it alone."

The steps bent under her weight, and Beth expected them to collapse beneath Clark, but they reached the porch, and he unlocked the door. The four-room house was completely devoid of furniture. There wasn't even a curtain at the windows. A worse scene of desolation Beth had never seen.

None of the day's outside warmth had penetrated the walls, and Beth shivered.

"I should never have come back to Warner Hollow."

Clark wrapped his arms around her and pulled her close. She laid her head on his shoulder.

"Think of the good memories, Bethie. Don't dwell on the sad times."

For a moment, all Beth could hear was the nightly sound of her father's troubled breathing, the quick choking sounds he made in his sleep while she lay trembling in the next room, wondering if he would die before morning.

"There are good memories," she murmured into the warmth of Clark's shoulder. "My daddy loved me devotedly. That's one reason my half siblings resented me—he gave me everything he could possibly afford, called me 'baby' to his dying day, and was proud of everything I did. Mom didn't show her emotions as readily, but she saw to my needs, prepared tempting foods, and tried to instill some common sense in me that I wouldn't have had if she hadn't exerted some discipline to make up for Daddy's spoiling."

"It's warmer outside—shall we go out?"

They stepped into a backyard littered with debris. Only the pump reminded her of the days when she'd lived here.

"I wish I had one memento of my childhood," Beth said. "I don't have anything that belonged to either of my parents. Immediately after their funeral, Grandmother Blaine took me away, so I suppose the other children removed everything before the property sold."

Humming a tune from one of the hymns they'd sung at church, Clark gazed around the hollow. "I know it's in a sorry state now, and probably has been since you can remember, but I can see real possibilities in having a home here—at least a summer home. With some money, this could be made into a pleasant place."

Beth shrugged her shoulders. "Maybe so, but my parents didn't have any money."

She pointed to a hill behind the house. "Let's climb up there. I used to have a playhouse under a rock ledge. I spent my most pleasant times there."

It was a steep climb, and both of them were breathing deeply before they reached the alcove where she used to play.

Panting, Beth said, "As I remember, I used to run up this hillside. I didn't get much exercise when I was in school—I'll have to do something about that."

"Shriver Mining has a gym for their employees at the main offices, but you won't be able to take advantage of that." He took her hand to pull her up the few remaining yards.

Her hideaway didn't look as if it had been disturbed since she had last played there, for the large, rocky overhang had protected the alcove from the elements. Through the years the wind had carved smooth, deep hollows and honeycombed crevices in the sandstone cliffs. Empty birds' nests were wedged in some of the crannies.

A smile broke across Beth's face as she dropped to her knees in the sandy soil that covered the floor. From a small wooden table that her father had made, she lifted a toy cup and plate. A few cracked dishes that she had carried from the house were stacked on a wooden shelf. Lifting one of the plates, she exclaimed,

"Oh, look. This matches the dishes your mother used last night."

Clark hunkered down in the opening of the cave and watched Beth with an understanding smile as she touched the frame of a battered lawn chair.

"Often I came here to get away from the miserable situation in the house when Daddy was doing so poorly, and Mom was irritable because she couldn't do anything for him. I sat here for hours, looking out over the valley, dreaming of better days to come. Sometimes I traveled to faraway places while I read the books I'd borrowed from the school library."

"Was that when you decided you wanted to leave Kentucky?"

Beth nodded, wondering why visiting those foreign places didn't seem as important now as it had then.

"I suppose every child has dreams." Beth sat gingerly in the old chair, wondering if it would support her weight. "What did you dream about, Clark?"

"I dreamed of going away, too, but I wanted to be a great athlete. I liked all sports, but mostly, I hoped I could play in major-league baseball."

"When did you lose your dream?"

"When my father was injured, and I began to feel a responsibility for my family. Actually, I don't think I lost the dream, but I decided that it was only a pipe dream. I realize now that God knew what was best for me—much better than I did. So many of the great athletes can't seem to handle the temptations of riches and they get into all kinds of trouble, so I'm happy that my dream didn't come true."

"But there are hundreds of great athletes who

haven't succumbed to temptation. We only hear about the few who do have trouble.''

"Yes, that's true, but I also realized that as long as I had peace of mind, I could find happiness anyplace. And as I grew older, I knew that everything I need for fulfillment is here.'' He tapped his breast.

Beth remembered his father's sermon text that morning. "For I have learned, in whatsoever state I am, therewith to be content.''

Clark moved closer to her and leaned his back against her knees. Reminiscing, he said, "When I was a child, I read a story in an old reader of my father's, and I thought of it this morning when Daddy was preaching.

"It was one of those 'Once upon a time' stories about a proud little hen who wasn't contented, and one day she started out to find the best thing in the world, which she thought was a pile of corn as big as a house. She met a squirrel and told him of her quest, and he joined her, but he said that the best thing in the world was a pile of nuts as high as a hill. The two traveled together until they encountered a duck who thought the best thing in the world was a muddy pond as large as the ocean.''

Beth's eyes twinkled and she ruffled his long, straight brown hair that was so close to her hand. "Are you trying to teach me a lesson?''

"Nope, just telling you a story. The duck decided to go along, and the three traveled most of the day, but they didn't find the corn, the nuts, or the pond. Disappointed, they started back home, and on the way, they reached the home of a woodchuck that was eating his supper. He looked happy and contented.''

Clark reached up and took Beth's hand, which still rested on his hair, and he clasped it to his shoulder.

"The woodchuck inquired where they had been, and when he was told that they'd been looking for the best thing in the world, the woodchuck said, 'You left it behind you early this morning.'

"'How could that be?' they cried, and the woodchuck said, 'Hen, you left it in the barnyard. Squirrel, you left it in the tree where your home is. Duck, you left it in your own pond.'

"'What was it?' the three searchers demanded.

"'Contentment,' the woodchuck replied as he took a bite out of a big red apple."

Beth laughed at the picture he had described.

"Your story has a lot of truth to it, and I'll admit that after the days we've spent canvasing this county and viewing the home life of some of the residents, I'm ready to concede that my childhood was a lot better than that of many people," Beth said. Clark squeezed her fingers gently as she added, "I'm inclined to believe that my greatest lack may be spiritual."

"You'll overcome that, Bethie. You've been running away from God all of your life, mostly because your parents didn't point you in the right direction, but when you turn to Him with an honest and penitent heart, God is ready and waiting to make you one of His own." He turned his head and kissed the hand that he held.

Beth stirred under his caress, then stood and looked around the cave.

"Would it be all right to take some of these things?" she asked.

"Help yourself. Representing Shriver Mining Company, I'll give them to you. They would be of no value to anyone else."

"No value to me, either, perhaps, but they are mementos of my childhood." She picked up the toy dishes and the best of the crockery. Looking up at the winter sun that was dropping closer to the horizon, Beth asked, "Shouldn't we be leaving?"

"I suppose so, but the sun will still be shining a long time up on the mountain."

After he helped Beth into the car, Clark stood for a few minutes glancing around the hollow with a speculative gleam in his eye, and she began to see the area from his perspective.

"I do feel a little sad that this place has gone out of the Warner family." She pointed to the family cemetery on the other side of the hollow. "It's almost as if we've forsaken our ancestors."

"Do you want to go up there before we leave?"

She shook her head. "I've had all I can handle today."

"I'll accompany you whenever you want to come back here. A few more visits and you'll feel at home once again."

When they reached the crest of the mountain, Clark parked the vehicle along the side of the road, saying, "Let's walk out to my old deer stand. It won't be dark for a couple of hours."

The hunting stand looked lonely when they came into the clearing where it was perched in the strong branches of the oak tree. Time had inflicted some ravages here, too, for several rungs of the ladder they had climbed to reach the platform had deteriorated and dropped to the ground.

Somewhat ruefully, Clark said, "I haven't been here for a long time, either. I, too, had some memories that I wanted to forget."

Beth lowered her head and wouldn't meet his gaze. Perhaps noting her downcast eyes, he continued, "But I had many pleasant memories, too." He walked close to her. "For instance, you were standing in that same spot the first time I kissed you. You'd better move, or I might take a notion to relive the past."

The magnetism of his presence nearly overwhelmed her, and for a moment, she was afraid. *Was she willing to start this all over again? If he kissed her, what would happen to her long-held hopes of leaving Kentucky?*

She lifted her head and met his searching brown eyes. "I haven't moved," she said softly.

That was invitation enough for Clark. Beth hadn't forgotten that former caress, either, and although their first kiss had been tender and breathtaking, it was nothing compared to the emotions that he stirred in her today. Clark had been a boy when he first kissed her, but now he was a man—a man with an unfailing love that was hers for the taking. All she had to do was accept it; but was she ready for it yet? She didn't know.

* * *

Two months from the day Beth had returned to Kentucky, the clinic opened, amid high praise from Milton Shriver for her quick and efficient work. She insisted that much of the success was due to Dr. Andrews and Clark. At first she had been frightened by the responsibility she had been given, but she was pleased with her achievements, and as work on the clinic progressed, Beth's enthusiasm for the project had increased.

Flyers had been prepared by the company and inserted in the county newspaper announcing that opening day would be March 15. The clinic would be open four days each week from nine to five, with a doctor on duty each Thursday afternoon. The clinic was closed on Fridays, but open on Saturday mornings. Beth was to work five days a week, but a nurse from the local hospital would staff the clinic when it was necessary for her to be away on a home confinement, or when she attended monthly staff meetings in Lexington. The flyer carried Beth's picture and a note on her accreditation, but in spite of the glowing publicity the company had given her, Beth had always heard that "a prophet was without honor in his own country." She questioned whether the people of Harlan County would want to trust their health to one of their own.

She wondered about that even more when, the day before the clinic opened, she received a visit from her sister, Luellen.

Beth was in the kitchen preparing her supper when the bell on the entrance door to the clinic rang. Surely no one would be coming a day early.

She popped the casserole that Anna Randolph had taught her to make into the oven, and lowered the temperature in case the visit was a lengthy one. When Beth unlocked the door, at first she didn't recognize the woman standing on the step.

"Well, aren't you going to ask me to come in?" The complaining, harsh tone of the voice left no doubt as to the identity of her visitor.

"Come in, Luellen." She opened the door, and her sister stalked into the room. Beth decided that the years hadn't been kind to Luellen, for as she waited for her sister to indicate the reason for the visit, Beth noticed that her face was etched with deep lines, per- haps from fatigue or worry—her hair was unkempt, and her clothing was not only worn, but unclean.

While Beth inspected her sister, Luellen was taking in every aspect of the clinic, studying each detail of the waiting room and peering into the examination area. Not for the first time, Beth was grateful to the scholarship from Shriver Mining that had enabled her to escape the harsh life that Luellen had experienced.

"What may I do for you?" Beth asked at last.

"You can't do anything for me," Luellen snapped. "Since you've been here for two months and didn't see fit to call on your kin, I thought I'd come to see you."

Beth hesitated, for she didn't want to antagonize her, but on the other hand, she didn't want to be blamed for a slight that she hadn't intended. "Frankly, I didn't think I'd be welcome—you never had time for me in the past, and I didn't suppose you had changed."

"You always were too high-and-mighty for your relatives, and having this big job ain't going to make you any better."

Beth wished Clark could have been present to hear Luellen's tirade; then perhaps he would understand why she didn't want to settle down in this neighborhood.

"Of course, I'll stop by to see you if you want me to. How is your family? How are our brothers?"

"They're not living here anymore. They got in some sort of trouble—a bad business scheme—and they had to leave the county. I don't know where they are."

Hearing this, Beth felt only relief that she could avoid seeing her brothers, at least until she was established in her position.

"And my family is a trial to me," Luellen continued. "Joe is an alcoholic and spends all of his money on booze. The two little boys ain't old enough to cause trouble yet, but Shirley has gone wild. I can't do a thing with her, and Joe is no help."

"How old is Shirley now?" Beth asked, remembering her niece as a quiet child, one whom she had liked.

"She's sixteen, and wild as a deer."

Luellen stayed for an hour, ranting about her problems, the unpleasant neighbors, and the poor conditions at Shriver Mine No. 10 where her husband worked. Beth knew that to attain the spiritual condition she desired, she would have to make peace with her sister, but how could she? Reconciliation took two people. As she closed the door behind Luellen, Beth had a sympathetic thought for Joe and the children, who had to live with such a bitter, disillusioned woman. *What had made her that way?*

The first week was over, and Beth breathed deeply as she locked the door at noon on Saturday. Twenty-five patients had visited the clinic, and the only major case had been a man with a broken arm, who came while Dr. Andrews was in the office, much to Beth's relief. She had been calm enough all week, but she might have panicked if she had been confronted with the suffering man who needed immediate help.

A few of the patients were members of the church Abner Randolph pastored, and Beth saw them each Sunday. She was convinced that her friendship with the Randolphs had been an asset.

Beth had advised several prenatal patients, dispensed cold medicines, taken blood pressures and checked diabetes patients. Two of the pregnant women had come for examinations, and had consulted her about having their children born at home rather than at the hospital. Beth had worked out a schedule of diet and exercise for them.

From the company's point of view, she considered the venture a success, and she was looking forward to talking over the week's work with Clark, who had been gone for several days dealing with a company problem in western Kentucky. After having been with him so much for the past couple of months, she missed him. Clark had telephoned this morning, and she expected him momentarily. She tried to keep her pleasure from being apparent when he finally came, but judging from his warm smile and gentle hug around her shoulders, he wasn't making any secret of how much he had missed her.

"I've had an interesting week," she said. "I want to show you my report before I fax it to Mr. Shriver."

Beth had set up an office in the former master bedroom of the residence, and the company had provided her with the latest in computer equipment. She was also connected to the Internet, and she had found it relaxing in the evening to surf the Net. She was especially pleased that she had connected with the Society of Christian Midwives. Not only had she been encouraged when she read about the techniques they employed and their solutions to problems they had experienced, but her faith in God had been strengthened when she learned how much these women depended on prayer during their ministry to pregnant women. Inspired by their stories, she had at last accepted God as the supreme authority in her life, and she was excited at how much peace that had brought to her heart. She wanted to tell Clark about it, too, and she knew he would want to hear that first.

"What's happened to you, Bethie?" were his first words. "You look radiant."

"I've finally accepted God and His will for my life."

"Well, praise the Lord! Tell me about it."

"Come in the living room. I've made a cake for you. You can eat while I talk." As she cut a slice of the cake and placed it on a plate, she said, "You know I've been reading my Bible and praying for guidance, but the big breakthrough came when I met other midwives on the Internet. When I learned how much those women were guided by God in their work, I knew that I could never succeed in what I'm doing without His leadership. I bowed my head there at the computer desk and asked Him into my life.''

Clark drew her into his arms. ''That's the most wonderful news you could have told me. So one of my prayers has been answered. I'm still waiting eagerly for you to tell me that the other one has been answered, too.''

She knew what he meant, and she smiled. ''Not today, sorry.'' And looking into his dear, hopeful expression, she did regret that she couldn't give him the commitment he longed for.

''Soon?''

''I don't know yet, Clark.''

He accepted her reply with his usual equanimity, then turned the conversation to other matters. They spent an hour looking over her weekly records. Clark asked a few questions, but finally he said, ''I'm impressed with your work as well as the response to the project. There's a need for this type of service, and I sincerely believe that you are the person who can give it. The fact that people kept coming after the first day or two indicates to me that the word got around that you were okay.''

Beth shook her head. ''I don't think it had that much to do with me. Dr. Andrews has an excellent reputation, and he's a good doctor. I worked with some of the best when I was in training, and he's very competent. His support of my work has convinced other people.''

"I agree that Dr. Andrews is greatly respected here, but I believe your compassion has a lot to do with it. Your spiritual gifts may very well be encouragement and empathy. One of the things that made me love you when you were just a girl was the way you sympathized with others and wanted to help them. That's a wonderful gift to receive."

"I don't know what you mean by 'spiritual gifts.'"

"Everyone has certain spiritual gifts—some people think of them as abilities or talents—but the kind I'm talking about come from God. We're content when we exercise those gifts, and that's what you've been doing this week. You're happier right now than I've ever known you to be, and that's because you're fulfilling your purpose in life."

"You may be right. I hadn't thought about it—I've been too busy to think."

"Mr. Shriver is going to be pleased with the report."

"I'll fax it this afternoon, so he'll have it when he comes to work on Monday morning."

"Have you had any night callers?"

"Nothing. Except for your calls, the phone rarely rings."

"What do you want to do this evening?"

"Do you have anything in mind?"

"Yes. Ray Gordon's band is playing at a restaurant in Hazard tonight. Would you like to go hear them?"

"Sounds like fun. Will Pam be there?"

"Probably—since she often goes to see them if they play in this area."

"Yes, I want to go with you. You can watch the

ball game on television while I finish my book work and fax the report to Lexington.''

Beth had almost completed her work when she heard a car drive into the parking lot, and she finished an entry about her last patient before she went to unlock the door. One of her maternity patients had missed an appointment this morning, so perhaps she was arriving now. Beth peered out the window to see a new tan sports car in the lot. None of her clients owned such a classy vehicle, and she hoped it wasn't a salesman calling on Saturday. Somewhat irritated, she opened the door.

''Hello, Beth. Remember me?''

Alex Connor!

''Well, of course,'' Beth said hesitantly, wishing that Clark wasn't in the apartment. ''Come in. How did you find me?''

Alex bustled into the room, took Beth's hands and leaned forward to kiss her. She turned her head and the caress landed on her cheek.

''If you aren't a sight for sore eyes. I've missed you, Beth.''

Beth withdrew her hands and waved Alex to a seat in the reception room. She perched on the edge of a desk.

''How did you know where to find me?'' she asked again.

''I stopped by Pam Gordon's house, and she gave me a rundown on what you've been doing. I can't believe that you've had time to graduate from college.''

"One can do lots of things in four years. Where have you been since you left Kentucky?"

"I was sent to Peru, and talk about being buried alive! I really experienced 'life's other side'! You can't imagine the poverty of that country. It was a relief to return to the U.S."

Beth looked down at her foot that was dangling carelessly a few inches above the floor. "Is it so backward that they don't have mail dispatches to the States?"

Alex didn't comprehend her meaning at first, but then he flushed slightly and laughed uproariously. "That's a good one. I'm not a letter writer, Beth, and besides, I didn't suppose I would be gone more than a year when I left Kentucky. Time just slipped away from me, but now I'm in the States for six months with the Department of International Development, traveling in the southeastern states to enlist investment in Peru and other developing nations."

"That sounds interesting."

"It is. I was in Lexington yesterday, and I decided that I wanted to look you up."

"I'm flattered."

Alex glanced at her. "Say, you aren't sore at me because I haven't kept in touch, are you?"

"Not at all. You didn't make any promise to do that."

"Good. I want to take you out for dinner this evening. What time can you be ready?"

Beth heard Clark's step in the doorway behind her, and she turned toward him. "Clark, this is Alex Connor, a friend from my high-school days. Alex, this is..." Beth wasn't sure how to introduce Clark and quickly said, "This is my co-worker, Clark Randolph."

Clark observed Alex closely, and as if she could read his thoughts, Beth sensed that Clark's mind quickly reverted to her graduation, knowing that he had never forgotten the man she had chosen over him that night. But if he was disturbed, he didn't show it. He held out a hand to Alex, who rose to shake hands with him.

"I didn't mean to interrupt, Beth. I'll go back to my ball game."

"No, sit down. Alex is representing the foreign service in this area again, and he's visiting people he knew when he was here before."

"But only for six months," Alex said, a broad smile lighting his handsome features, "for I've landed a whale of an assignment. I'm being sent to Paris for five years. I can hardly wait. I intend to see the whole of Europe during my stay in France."

"That sounds like a great opportunity," Clark said.

Alex turned to Beth. "How about it, Beth? Will you have dinner with me? We can eat early—I have to go back to Lexington tonight."

Was she tempted? Beth didn't really know, but she shook her head. "Clark and I have plans for the evening."

Alex smiled in Clark's direction. "I'm sure Mr. Randolph will excuse you from your appointment, since we haven't seen each other for years."

Without meeting Beth's eyes, Clark said, "I'll leave that decision up to the lady."

Beth shook her head determinedly. "No, thank you, Alex. Perhaps I can take a rain check on your invitation."

"Sure—I'll telephone before I drop by the next time."

"That would be much better. I do have a rather full schedule, and it's taking lots of time to get the clinic established."

Alex stepped jauntily, whistling merrily, as he left the clinic and went to his car. Clark watched Beth, instead of Alex.

"I would have understood if you'd wanted to visit with him."

"I deserted you once for Alex Connor, and I've suffered for it ever since. Besides, I'm not sure I would have gone with him, even if you and I weren't going to Hazard. He can't walk out of my life without a word for years and expect me to change my plans at a snap of his fingers. But to give him credit, neither of us had made a commitment to the other, so we were both free to do what we wanted."

Clark locked the outer door, and started picking up magazines and putting them in the racks. He pulled the draperies, after hanging a Closed sign in the window.

"Sounds to me as if he can give you everything that you want in life."

"Yes, it does, doesn't it? That's assuming, of course, that I still want what I did when I knew Alex before. I've changed a lot since that time." The surprise of seeing Alex was still in her mind, and she didn't want to discuss him with Clark—especially when she herself didn't know what she thought about Alex. "Let's get ready to head for Hazard—I'm looking forward to getting away from my work for a few hours."

Alex wasn't mentioned for the rest of the evening.

Since Harlan and Hazard weren't connected by a direct route, Clark and Beth left by four o'clock so they would be at the restaurant before the music started. During the week, the restaurant catered to the needs of the local residents, but on Saturday night, the manager moved out a few tables, set up a portable platform, and invited popular musicians to entertain his guests. Clark had telephoned for reservations, which had been a good idea, since the room was filling up rapidly when they arrived.

"I asked them to seat us near Pam, if she's here," Clark explained as they entered the dining room, and Beth spotted her at a small table near the stage. Pam was watching for them, and she waved gaily. "Over here. I've saved places for you."

Four-year-old Grace sat on a booster seat, and she dropped her head shyly when Beth and Clark arrived at the table.

Clark patted Grace on the head. "Hey! Why so much shyness? You know who I am."

Grace sneaked a peek at Clark but hid her face against her mother's arm.

"Oh, don't knock a good thing," Pam said, laughing. "She'll soon be lively enough."

The menu choice on Saturday night was simple, in order to serve the large crowd quickly. The choices were chicken or baked steak, served with a baked potato and coleslaw, and apple or cherry pie for dessert.

While they waited for the meal to be served, Pam plied Beth with questions about her work, and Clark enticed Grace to his side by offering her a dollar.

"Well, no wonder you can't get a wife," Pam teased, "if you have to buy a female's affection."

"Oh, I'm not faring too badly," Clark retorted. "I'm keeping company with the three prettiest women in the house tonight."

It soon became difficult to carry on a conversation seated as they were near the stage where the five-member band was tuning instruments. Ray, the director of the band, was also the banjo player, and the other musicians played the fiddle, mandolin, six-string guitar, and bass, although Pam explained, "Most of the guys can play all of the instruments, but they excel in one particular one. I personally think that Ray can play the mandolin better than the banjo, but who am I to argue music with my husband? The only music I can produce is on the radio, and even there I have static."

The crowd quieted when Ray Gordon stepped to the mike and thumped a few chords on the banjo. As the band played the old favorite, "Orange Blossom Special," featuring the fiddle, which Beth remembered hearing at miners' rallies, the floor vibrated with enthusiastic toe-tapping from the audience. Ray was a handsome man with a neat, tapered beard glistening with streaks of gray. His slender, six-foot-tall body was enhanced by a dark gray suit, blue shirt, and white tie. He glanced at Pam and smiled, and Beth detected the love that still marked their marriage. *Pam had found love and contentment in Kentucky; could she do likewise with Clark?*

After the first number, Ray announced, "Our program tonight is dedicated to Bill Monroe, native Kentuckian, who, in 1939, founded a band named the Blue Gray Boys, and they created the particular kind of music that became known as bluegrass music and gave Monroe and his boys a spot at the Grand Ole Opry."

Ray went on to explain that bluegrass was a highly disciplined American art form, which had gone through some changes through the years, but it had never changed from being an ensemble of stringed instruments. Beth hadn't thought of Monroe's music as being a part of her heritage, but she decided it must be, since Monroe had taken Scotch-Irish dance tunes, ballads, blues, and hymns—all types of music that she had known in her youth—and put them together in a new way.

Ray's band always closed its concerts with a hymn sing, and the refrain of one song rang in her ears as they traveled homeward. "God holds the future in His hands, and every heart He understands; on Him depend."

If God understood her heart, why couldn't He reveal to her what the future held for her and Clark?

Clark didn't bring Beth home until well after midnight, so she was less than pleased when she awoke before four in the morning and couldn't get back to sleep. But then, hardly a night passed that she didn't awaken to think about her future, especially as it concerned Clark. Were her childhood dreams really so important when compared to her love for Clark?

Chapter Six

The next morning after they returned from church, Clark grinned at her. "I have to go into Harlan—I bought a present for you, and I want to deliver it before we have lunch. Incidentally, I'll stop at a deli and order some food."

"A gift that you couldn't have brought when you came this morning?"

"You'll see soon enough," he said with a mysterious look.

Beth made some coffee while she waited for Clark to return. When he finally knocked and Beth opened the door, a golden-brown streak bounded past her, almost pushing her over.

"What was that?" she screeched.

Clark whistled, and a dog with a dense fawn coat covering its smoothly muscled body ran into the kitchen from the living room. The animal was at least two feet tall.

"This is Ranger, your bodyguard," Clark said with

a satisfied smile. "With Ranger around, I don't think you'll be bothered by night prowlers. I've been worried about you alone here at night. I ordered Ranger especially for you," he said proudly, but Beth eyed the dog warily.

"But, Clark, I don't have time to take care of a dog. Besides, as big as he is, I'll need protection from *him*."

Clark patted the strong shoulders and massive head of the golden-coated animal. "Not at all. These canines are gentle and make excellent watchdogs. According to his trainer, he will be a mild and affectionate companion."

The dog looked up at Beth, the black mask on his face accenting keen, intelligent eyes. His hopeful expression made Beth weaken, but she continued to protest.

"He's mighty large for such a small apartment. He'll have to stay outdoors."

Clark shook his head. "No—to be any help to you, he'll need to be indoors. Please promise me that you'll keep him, Bethie. I have to go back to Lexington for the week, and I'll be more comfortable if you have some protection."

Beth flushed from the intense concern in Clark's eyes. All he had to do was call her "Bethie" in that tone of voice, and it instantly melted her resistance.

"Okay, I'll keep him until you come back. On trial only, mind you." Treading softly, the dog walked proudly into the living room, where he could easily look out the picture window.

Beth laughed. "He's even bigger than I thought—

perhaps such a big dog *will* be a deterrent to crime if a burglar sees him."

"And I might as well warn you—he'll get bigger. He's only six months old."

"How much do I owe you for my bodyguard?"

"More than you can afford to pay. I've charged it to Shriver Mining. You can't live out here without some protection, and they should pay for it."

"What kind of dog is he?"

"A Great Dane—they're magnificent animals, probably descended from an ancient breed once kept on princely estates in Europe to hunt wild boars. Since you've agreed to keep him, I'll bring in his supplies."

He carried in a feeding dish, a huge bag of dog food, and a large, soft, concave pallet as Ranger's bed. "There's a leash in that box—you'll need to walk him every day, and he has to be restrained until he becomes used to the place."

After they ate their deli lunch, Clark had to leave for Lexington, and he took her hand and pressed it to his cheek and, with his other hand, ran his forefinger down the side of her face. Her eyes locked with his as he tipped her chin and kissed her softly on the lips before he left the room.

Beth stood quietly, listening to the sound of his vehicle leaving the parking lot, her hand pressed to her lips. The words that Abner had quoted in his sermon this morning reminded her of Clark: "How priceless is your unfailing love." Abner had explained that no one deserved the love God had displayed when He sent Jesus to die for the sins of all mankind. She believed that, and she also conceded that she didn't deserve the love that Clark showered on her. She wondered, short of marrying him, what else she could do to show how much she appreciated him.

She shook her head to clear her mind of disturbing thoughts, and said, "Well, dog, what am I going to do with you?" Amused, she saw that the dog was taking care of himself. He had pulled his bed to one corner of the living room, and was turning around and around on it to fit it to his shape. Head held high, he gripped his feeding dish in his mouth and carried it to a conspicuous spot on the kitchen floor. Then he placed his water bowl beside it. He looked expectantly at Beth.

She knelt on the floor. "Come here, Ranger," she said, and he perked up his ears at the sound of his name. "We'd better get acquainted. My name is Beth."

When the dog came to her side, he was at eye level with her. She put her arm around his smooth, golden shoulders, and he licked her face.

"Maybe I do need a companion, Ranger. We'll see how it works out, but you'll have to fend for yourself during the daytime. I'm too busy, and the clinic is off-limits to you," she added sternly.

Beth filled the dog's containers with water and food, and while she worked on her books in the clinic, she could hear Ranger slurping up the contents. The bowls were empty when she returned to the kitchen, and Ranger was asleep on his bed.

A pretty blond girl was the only one in the waiting room when Beth opened the door on Monday morning. With a smile, she ushered the girl into the examination room.

"Now what can I do for you?"

"I want to find out if I'm pregnant."

Beth was taken aback by the blunt statement. She glanced at the girl's hands—there was no wedding ring.

"How long do you suspect you've been pregnant?"

"Three months."

"I'll examine you, but there are tests that you can give yourself."

"I took one of those and tested positive. I'm almost sure that I'm pregnant, but I wanted to get your opinion. When my mother finds out, she will kick me out of the house, and I have to make some plans before she learns about it."

Beth handed her a long gown. "Go into the dressing room, remove your garments and put this on."

Silently, the girl took the gown, and Beth turned away to get the items she would need for the examination. She was certainly calm about it, Beth thought.

After the exam, while the girl was getting dressed, Beth filled out the record of her examination, and when her patient returned, Beth said, "I need your name for my records."

For the first time, she hesitated. "Shirley Rupe."

Beth started to write the name down, but she lifted her head swiftly.

"Rupe?"

A sardonic look crossed Shirley's face. "Luellen Rupe is my mother."

Beth laid down her pen. "And my sister."

Shirley nodded. "And she doesn't like either one of us. As a matter of fact, she doesn't like anyone. Dad told her once that she was 'soured on the world.' I don't blame him for drinking as he does."

"Well, Shirley, both of us have problems. You *are* pregnant, and although I'll do what I can to help you, Luellen will be quite angry that you've come to me."

"I know that, but I've heard good things about you, and somehow I felt that I could trust you with my secret."

"Certainly, you can. I don't divulge professional information, but it can't remain a secret much longer. It's my opinion that you're *more* than three months' pregnant. I assume you have no thought of marriage."

Shirley shook her head. "I don't want to shock you, but without going into details, let me say that I don't know who the father is."

Beth's dismay must have shown on her face, for Shirley said, "Don't let it upset you. I was old enough to know what I was getting into. Now that I'm sure of my condition, I'll apply for assistance for unwed mothers. A friend of mine is in the same situation, and we think we can share an apartment and help each other."

"Are you still in school?"

"Yes, and I figure I can finish this year at least."

"I wish I could have spared you this, Shirley."

Shirley shrugged her shoulders. "Can you deliver my baby when the time comes?"

"Yes. I'm a certified midwife."

Shirley nodded. "I guess you're really my aunt. What should I call you?"

"'Beth' will do. You can't have any filial devotion to me when we've rarely seen one another."

"I've always wondered why my mother didn't like you."

"So have I. It really disturbed me when I was a child, but I finally became hardened to it. I've always thought it was because our father remarried, and I was a result of that marriage. Luellen said that my daddy spoiled me, and perhaps he did. At least, she seemed to think he paid more attention to me than he had to her. But regardless, I want you to think of me as a friend, and if Luellen does make you leave home, I'll try to do what I can to find a place for you."

Beth didn't have another patient for an hour after Shirley left, and she lowered her head to her folded hands on the desk in front of her.

God, she murmured. *How thankful I am that I'm on speaking terms with You now. Shirley needs help, and I don't know how to pray for her. What can I do to help in this situation, and what can I do to turn her life around, so she won't get into this condition again?*

She prepared herself for an answer, which didn't come right away, possibly because her mind was too full of the past. Her prayer life was so new that she still expected immediate results when she prayed, but Clark had told her that wouldn't always be the case.

Shirley was the same age she had been when Clark wanted to marry her. If she had become his wife, she might have had a child within the year. Could she put herself in Shirley's place and understand how the girl must be feeling? Beth knew that she was fortunate that Clark was the boy who had loved her, or she might have been in the same condition as Shirley, although Beth suspected that Shirley was more worldly-wise than she herself had ever been.

Ranger proved to be a tractable dog, and Beth was glad to have his company. Sometimes, she would awaken and hear the dog pacing back and forth in her apartment. Most of the night, though, he lay beside her bed, and slept on his own pallet during the day. Although she didn't anticipate any trouble, it was reassuring to have the friendly beast with her.

Beth had wondered if she would ever see Alex again, but he telephoned on Wednesday afternoon, asking her out for dinner. She accepted the invitation, wishing that she'd taken time to buy some new clothes, but she put on an ankle-length ice-green shirt-waist dress and was pleased with her appearance. Her hair was longer than she usually wore it, but she'd been too busy to go to the beauty parlor for a trim, so after a shampoo she brushed her hair forward around her oval face.

Since the weather was moderating, she extracted a lightweight beige coat from a box of summer clothing. After she'd pressed out the wrinkles, she decided that she looked good enough for a date with a former flame.

Alex had changed a lot in four years, Beth decided as the evening progressed. Or was she the one who had changed?

It wasn't difficult to entertain Alex, for he did most of the talking—mainly about his exploits in Peru— and while Beth did find his conversation interesting, she decided that he was self-centered. They went to a steak house for the meal, and as she sat across from him, listening to his voice, she couldn't resist comparing him to Clark. She'd made the same comparison when she had first met Alex.

At that time, Clark had come off second best. She remembered she had compared Alex's smooth, tapered fingers and well-groomed nails to Clark's rough touch and broken, stained fingernails. Alex had been immaculately dressed in a suit and tie, while the only time she'd seen Clark dressed up had been the night he'd taken her to the prom, and he had been obviously ill at ease in his new clothes. Conversation with Alex had been uplifting and educational, opening for Beth new horizons far exceeding her wildest dreams. Clark, on the other hand, at that time had no firsthand knowledge about anything outside Harlan County, and during their infrequent meetings, Beth and Clark had spent more time in silence than they had in conversation.

So how did the two men compare now? Clark's hands were no longer rough, and his nails were neatly manicured, though they were strong, competent hands, still possessing the strength garnered during his days in the mine. Alex's hands were small, unused to manual labor, and they were pasty white. Alex still looked as if he'd stepped from the pages of a fashion magazine, and although Clark wore business suits quite often, the fine cut of his clothing couldn't disguise his muscular physique.

But the greatest contrast between the two was in their inner strength. Alex possessed a drive to further his personal career at any cost. He apparently didn't think he needed other people to gain his ends. Whereas Clark wasn't concerned about his own advancement, and showed absolutely no pride in the phenomenal jump he'd made from the coal mines to the corporate office. And while Alex was self-centered, Clark had a concern for others that was far-reaching in its effect.

And what about Beth Warner? How did she compare to the girl who had been so enamored of Alex? When she'd been associated with Alex before, she had completely forgotten her interest in being of service to others. If she had gone with Alex instead of attending college, would her dream have been totally subjugated to Alex's ambitions?

Beth believed that if she put forth an effort now, she could have Alex, for he made it plain that he'd thought of her often while he was gone. He could give her the material things she had coveted; but were those things more valuable to her than what she could have as Clark's wife? *If she had to choose between the two men, what would her choice be?*

When they reached the door of her apartment, she heard the patter of Ranger's big feet as he ran to the door. At his low growl, she spoke, "It's all right, Ranger," but she could sense his watchful stance as he guarded the entrance.

"May I come in?" Alex asked.

After a slight hesitation, she said, "No, I think not, Alex. It's late and I have a busy day tomorrow. But thank you for a lovely evening."

"May I see you again when I'm back in this area?"

"Give me a call when you return, and I can tell you then."

Alex leaned forward and kissed her, but when he would have embraced her, Beth slipped from his grasp. She inserted her key in the lock and pushed past Ranger, who placed his body between her and Alex.

Laughing, Alex said, "You have a good watchdog, there. I guess I'd better mind my manners."

"Good night, Alex. Thanks for dinner."

Why had she hesitated to invite Alex into her apartment when Clark came and went as if he lived there? Did her reaction stem from her scant knowledge of Alex's character, or from her confidence in Clark's behavior?

Beth often visited Clark's family on Saturday nights and one evening she had asked Abner, "Could you tell me what caused the Warner-Randolph feud and what happened as a result of it? Daddy was always so irate when a Randolph was mentioned that I never could make any sense of his rantings."

Abner smiled. "I don't know much about it—seems the trouble started during the Civil War when the Randolphs had Unionist sentiments, and the Warners fought with the Confederacy. But I think our feud was more one of words than of actions. To my knowledge, there was never any violence similar to the famous feuds we've heard so much about."

"I don't care what my ancestors did. I have no quarrel with the Randolphs."

"Then let's be the generation that buries the feud,"

Abner replied. "I don't want you for my enemy, Beth."

"It would have been much easier in the early days when I first knew Clark, if we hadn't had to sneak around to see each other. I was afraid my daddy would find out. He always thought the Randolphs were his enemies—whether they were or not—and actually, I can't think of a single deed against him that could be blamed on the Randolphs."

"You'll have to overlook your father's prejudices, Beth," Abner advised. "His war record was an excellent one, but when he became sick and couldn't live a normal life, he dwelled on his difficulties. He had to hate someone for his health problems, and the Randolphs were closer than his wartime enemies."

"You make me feel better about him. I did resent his attitude."

While Beth was on good terms with Clark's parents, she thought that his sisters resented her at first, but slowly they were accepting her. In appearance, both girls had Clark's characteristics, but Sallie was quiet like her mother, while Mary Lynn had the same outgoing personality as her brother. Once, when Beth had commented that she wasn't a good cook, Mary Lynn had quipped, "You'd better learn—Clark is a big eater."

Beth's face had crimsoned, and Anna had frowned at her older daughter, but the matter hadn't been pursued.

Sallie had stayed with Beth for a few days when the roads were snow-covered and she wanted to be close to her work in Harlan, so as far as Clark's family was concerned, Beth knew they wouldn't offer any objection if she agreed to marry Clark, and many times she thought longingly of having a loving family around her. That would be enough incentive to become a Randolph, even if she didn't love Clark.

Several weeks passed and Beth didn't hear from her niece, Shirley, and she wondered how the girl was getting along. By this time, Luellen should have suspected that her daughter was pregnant. And then one morning when Beth returned from a twelve-hour home birth, she found Shirley sitting on the back steps. The girl stood stiffly as Beth parked her car, and she wondered if she had been there all night. Despite the huge jacket she wore, her pregnancy was obvious.

"Well," Shirley said to Beth's questioning glance. "I couldn't hide it any longer, and she ordered me to leave the house."

Unlocking the door and fending off Ranger's joyous welcome, Beth said, "Come on in, Shirley. Have you had anything to eat? How long have you been here?"

"I've been here since midnight, but no matter—I'm not hungry."

"How did you get here?"

"A friend brought me."

"Take off your jacket, and I'll prepare some breakfast for you. There's milk in the refrigerator."

Beth placed some toast and a fresh peach on the table for Shirley and made a cup of coffee for herself.

"Now what?" Beth questioned.

Shirley shook her head, and even though she spoke

in a steady voice, Beth could detect concern in her eyes.

"I don't know. If you'll let me stay with you for a few days, I'll figure out something."

"If you can be content with a cot in one of the examining rooms, you're welcome to stay."

"A cot is better than sleeping on the ground. I won't ask any of my friends to take me in because their parents wouldn't like it. They'll think I'm not fit company for their children, and I'm probably not. I've been pretty wild."

"Why, Shirley?"

"To lash out at my mother, I suppose. The counselor at school had some sessions with me when she learned I was pregnant, and she says that I've been lacking love, and that I was doing the things I've done because I wanted attention. Does that make sense to you?"

"Yes, it does. I felt the same way when I was a teenager, but I didn't react the way you did. I'm willing to help you, but I'm counting on you to mend your ways. I think you owe me that consideration."

"Do you think I like behaving the way I have for the past year? Lots of times, I can't even face myself in the mirror. I'd like to change, but I'll be honest—I don't think I will if I stay around here. My reputation is too bad, and I'll be tempted every day by my friends who know what I've been and won't understand why I want to change."

"Then you'll need to go away. There are homes for unwed mothers where you can receive care and counseling while you finish your education. Would you be willing to do that?''

"Where?''

Beth shook her head. "I don't have any idea, but I'm sure Clark Randolph can locate one in Lexington.''

"I'll appreciate whatever help you give me, and I'll do my best to go straight—that's all I can promise.''

"You said before that you didn't know who the father is. Surely you have some idea.''

"I suppose we could find out by DNA testing, but what good would it do? Even if I found out, it would be someone about my own age, and what future would I have if I married a boy like that? Although it may not be obvious, I really would like to make something of my life.''

Shirley couldn't have said anything else that would have given Beth more reason to help her. *How often had she voiced those same sentiments when she was a girl?*

"It's going to be difficult to care for a child by yourself.''

"I've thought a lot about it and I guess I'll have to give it up for adoption. For the child's own sake, that's the only way, don't you think?'' Shirley didn't look at Beth when she made the comment.

"Probably so, but we'll check out all the possibilities. Right now, I have to get ready to see patients. I assume you don't have any clothing.''

"Nothing but what I'm wearing.''

"We're nearly the same size so I'll give you a nightgown and a change of clothes for tomorrow, but you'll have to get your own clothes from Luellen fairly soon.''

"If I can get in touch with my dad, he'll bring my clothes to me. He doesn't assert himself very often, but when he does, Mom pays attention. I'll try to contact him at his favorite bar when he leaves work today.''

When she had a lull in the morning's patients, Beth dialed Clark's office number, hoping that she could contact him. Her heart flooded with relief when he answered. She seldom telephoned him, and he was obviously pleased, but would he remain so when he found out the reason for her call?

They exchanged greetings, and he asked, "Everything okay there?''

"Not really. You remember I told you about my niece, Shirley Rupe? Her mother has thrown her out of the house, and she's here with me.''

"What!''

"The girl doesn't have any other place to go. I was hoping you could help me. She wants to get away from Harlan County to bear the child, and then offer it for adoption. I'm inclined to believe that's best for her and the baby. Do you know of any homes for unwed mothers in Lexington?''

"I'm sure there are such places, but I'll have to do some investigating. I don't like to have you troubled with such a situation.''

"It's part of my job. She's the daughter of one of Shriver's miners, so even if Shirley wasn't kin, I'd still feel obligated to help anyone who had a similar problem. If we can keep her away from her mother, I think she'll try to go straight.''

"Are you prepared for your sister's wrath?" Clark asked, and Beth sensed that he was smiling.

"No, I'm not. She's always intimidated me."

"I'll be in touch in a few days."

That night, Beth drove Shirley to a bar in Harlan, and waited while she went inside to look for her father. After a few minutes, Shirley returned, followed by a man whom Beth recognized as Joe Rupe, although she hadn't seen him since her parents' funeral. Shirley got in the back seat, and Joe sat in the front beside Beth. She shook hands with him.

"Beth, I'm glad to see you doing so well. You had a rough time of it as a child, but you've overcome the past. I do appreciate what you're doing to help Shirley. Maybe she can turn out all right, too."

"I'll do my best to help her, but she'll need your support, too, Joe."

"I didn't know that Luellen had pushed Shirley out. And if she wants to, I'll see that she goes back home and stays there. I'm the one who provides for my family, and I'm not going to abandon my own daughter. I won't let Luellen do it either."

"I'm not sure it's a good idea for her to live with her mother."

"I'm sure it isn't, but she can stay if she wants to."

"I'd rather leave, Dad," Shirley said tearfully from the back seat.

"Well, I'll see that you get your clothes and anything else that belongs to you. Beth, if you can bring her to the house tomorrow after I get home from work, I'll be there and see that she gets all her things.''

"All right," Beth agreed. "We'll come about six o'clock.''

"Be sure you're there, Dad," Shirley said fearfully.

Joe patted Shirley on the shoulder before he got out of the car. "I won't fail you this time, Shirley."

Beth slept restlessly that night, dreading the encounter with Luellen. She was on edge all the next day, as was Shirley. As they approached the Rupe home that evening, Shirley whispered more than once, "I hope Dad didn't forget. If he isn't at home, we'll just drive on by."

Beth breathed a thank-you prayer when they pulled off the road in front of the Rupe trailer and saw Joe sitting on the porch. They had brought along several boxes and Beth helped carry them to the porch.

Joe touched his hat. "It might be best if you stay in the car, Beth. I can't protect two of you at once. I'll carry Shirley's boxes to your car."

Beth couldn't believe that Luellen would actually harm her own daughter, but Joe had lived with her sister for a long time. No sooner had he and Shirley entered the house than Luellen bolted out the door, running down the steps toward Beth, with Joe at her heels. Beth hurriedly got into her car and locked the door. Joe caught his wife before she reached Beth's car and stopped her in her tracks.

Luellen struggled, but when she couldn't break her husband's hold, she shouted scathing insults at Beth, ending with, "You took my daddy away from me. Now you're trying to steal my daughter!"

Before Beth's birth had John Warner showered on Luellen the love that he'd given to Beth, and from then on, ignored his older daughter's need for love? That may have been true, but Beth wished Luellen would understand that if anyone was to be blamed for the situation, it was their father, not Beth.

Beth rolled down the window of her car. "I know you're angry and disappointed with Shirley but she needs help right now. I took her in rather than have her sleeping on the street. I'm only trying to help her get her life back on track."

When Luellen continued to scream at Beth, Joe sternly led her back inside the house. As the front door closed, Beth leaned her head on the steering wheel. Why did each encounter with her sister cause such a conflict? She was weary of it all—no wonder she wanted to leave the area. But did she really want to leave? Leave Clark and her work at the clinic, which was challenging and satisfying to her? It was the first time she had felt real doubts about going. She quickly brushed all thoughts about the question aside and focused on Shirley and the current crisis.

Joe and Shirley carried five boxes from the house, and Beth stored them in the trunk and on the back seat. Shirley was crying when she got into the car. Joe shook hands with Beth.

"What are you aiming to do?" he asked.

"Clark Randolph is looking for a residence for unwed mothers in Lexington where Shirley can have her baby. She'll get counseling there, too, and they'll help her continue her education and make plans for herself.''

"Clark is a good guy—you can depend on what he tells you.''

"If you call the clinic occasionally, I'll keep you aware of what's going on. I'm sure you'll want to keep in touch with Shirley once she goes to Lexington— maybe visit her there, as well. She needs you now, Joe.''

"Yes, I can see now how I've let her down. But I'm going to do better,'' he promised soberly.

Shirley continued to sob as Beth drove away, and Beth laid her hand on the girl's shoulder.

"I've been miserable there,'' Shirley sobbed, "but it's the only home I've ever had.... And I'm afraid of the future.''

"That's exactly the way I felt when I left Kentucky and went away to nursing school, but if I hadn't had the courage to break the familiar ties, I wouldn't have the career and real choices in life I have now. Shriver Mining does a lot of good things for its employees' families, and I imagine Clark will be able to work out some way for you to finish your education.''

"You like Clark, don't you?''

"Very much. He's a good friend.''

That night, since there was a possibility that she might go away soon, Shirley decided not to return to school. Beth didn't try to change her mind, for she figured that they would hear from Clark soon. The next day while Beth was in the clinic, Shirley cleaned the apartment, and Beth was delighted with the thorough cleaning, for with keeping the clinic spotless, she didn't have time for her own quarters. To Luellen's credit, she must have taught Shirley to work hard.

Clark telephoned the following night. "I have a place for her," he said. "It's a strict facility, and if she tries any hanky-panky, they'll put her out right away. But they will take care of her through childbirth, arrange for the adoption, and keep her on until she finishes her high-school work."

"That might be two years."

"Not there—she will be going to school steadily, and the students matriculate sooner than in a public school."

"What about expenses?"

"Shriver Mining will pay part of it, since she's an employee's daughter, but the place is funded by several church groups. She will have to be admitted by one of her parents."

"I'm sure Joe will do it."

"If you'll notify Joe, I'll arrange for him to get off work, and I'll come for Joe and Shirley on Friday morning to take them to Lexington. Okay?"

"Sounds great to me. And, thanks a lot, Clark."

That evening, Shirley telephoned the bar where her father was often found, and he agreed to take the trip to Lexington with them.

On the night before they left, Beth and Shirley had a long talk. Though she'd only known her niece for a short time, Beth felt close to the girl and concerned about her future. Shirley was afraid to go to Lexington and live entirely among strangers at the residence. She hadn't had a happy home life, but had never been any-where else. Beth tried to reassure her that the counselors there wanted to help her and would understand her problems. She might even make some friends among the other girls, who were all in the same situation, Beth reminded her. Shirley quietly considered everything Beth said and seemed a bit calmer by the time Beth promised she'd keep in touch and visit her when she could.

Finally Beth said to Shirley, "This may be the last chance you'll have to turn your life around. Please, don't waste it, Shirley."

"I'll try not to."

"It's going to take more than that. Clark said this facility is strict. I believe you're used to breaking the rules, but if you do it there, you'll be asked to leave."

"It won't be easy," Shirley said honestly.

"No. It won't be. But I think you can do it. I believe you are smart and can show a lot of determination if you apply yourself."

"Beth, all I can promise is that I'll try. I've never thought much of myself. Living with Luellen Rupe didn't do much to encourage my self-esteem, but I want to do better, make a good life for myself someday and I hope that I can.

When Clark came to pick Beth up for church the next Sunday, he said, "Shirley is settled into the residence, and she seems content enough. The girls do have some freedom—it won't be like living in jail, and I personally feel that Shirley will appreciate some discipline from people who have her best interests at heart. I felt sorry for Joe. He hated to leave her there, but he's happy to have her away from her mother."

"I'll try to visit her occasionally."

"Good. There are lots of places in Lexington that I want to take you to, so plan to stay overnight when you come, and I'll entertain you. You always rush back after our Friday staff meetings—we don't have any time together."

"I have to open the clinic on Saturday morning, so I don't have time to stay in Lexington overnight."

Beth had avoided spending much social time with Clark, for she didn't want to give him any false hopes about their future. If she saw him only when they were on company business, it would keep him from becoming hopeful. She didn't ever want to hurt him again.

As he drove slowly toward the church, Clark said, "I have a surprise for you. I've bought your father's property, and that tract of land on Randolph Mountain where I used to hunt."

Beth stared at him. "Why would you buy that property? And why would Milton Shriver want to sell it?"

"Shriver Mining owns hundreds of acres of land in eastern Kentucky. They'll never miss those few acres. Milton didn't believe the sale would interfere with any mining they might eventually do in the area."

"Why would you want such an isolated place?"

"I bought your father's property because I thought you felt badly about having the land go out of the family. Someday you might want to own it, Bethie. If so, you can have it, and I bought that parcel on Randolph Mountain because I have sentimental ties to it."

She looked at him tenderly and extended a hand to touch his cheek. He reached up and took her hand in his strong grasp and moved it to his lips. She knew by now that he only called her Bethie when his emotional stress was so great it threatened to smother him. Determined to keep control of her own emotions, which were more and more unruly when she was in Clark's presence, she steeled herself to speak calmly.

"I feel badly that you bought that property when I might never want to own it. You know I still haven't come to any decision about what I will do when my two years are completed. Clark, I don't want you to be hurt again."

"Bethie, you aren't under any obligation to me. The property is a good investment whether or not you want it."

She laughed gaily as a thought penetrated her mind. "My father would certainly be angry to know that a Randolph owned his ancestral home," she said jokingly.

"I don't think he'd mind once he knew that I bought it to please his daughter," Clark replied with a loving smile.

After church, Clark said, "I ordered a box lunch at the deli in town. Let's pick it up and picnic on Randolph Mountain or down in the hollow. I want to discuss renovation plans with you."

Beth shook her head. "It's your property—do what you want to do with it."

"A second opinion is always good. When you lived there, didn't you sometimes dream about how you would like to fix up the house to make it more comfortable?"

"Of course. Having water in the house and a bathroom topped the list. I don't know how many buckets of water I pumped and then carried into the house. And I always felt sorry that my mother had to pump water. She had a hard life.''

"The plumber is starting next week. Anything else?''

Beth couldn't help but grin at him. Clark always had a way of drawing her into his enthusiasm—no matter how she resisted.

"Okay, you win.'' She laughed. "Let's picnic at the house. And let's take Ranger along. The yard here doesn't give him much room for exercise.''

"Good idea. He can run anywhere he wants this afternoon.''

Chapter Seven

Clark grinned at the look of amazement on Beth's face when he turned onto a smooth, graded road leading up Randolph Mountain, and the improvement continued on down into the hollow. It was like a boulevard compared to what the road had always been.

"Who did all this work?" she asked in surprise.

"It's an advantage to have Shriver Mining equipment at your disposal. A lot of our machinery was at Shriver No. 10 Mine, so I asked the guys to do this grading before they moved on."

"It's the smoothest ride here I've ever had."

Clark parked in front of the house, and lifted a large bag out of the back of the vehicle. He unfastened Ranger's leash and let him jump to the ground. The dog yelped a few times, then bounded into the underbrush across the road. Clark gave Beth a folded blanket to carry.

"I just hope we can find him when we get ready to leave," Beth said.

She looked up at the cemetery, where lilacs, snow-balls, and azaleas were in bloom. A sweet smell wafted down to where they stood, and Beth smiled, remembering the days and nights when the entire hollow was fragrant with the aroma of blooming plants.

"I think I'm ready to go up to the cemetery now," she said softly. "The last time, I couldn't go."

"Shall we eat first?"

"Yes, but I will visit the graves before we leave."

"Let's go up to your playhouse. We can sit on the ledge and look down the hollow. There's a pretty view from there, especially this time of year."

"Yes, I remember."

When they reached the stone ledge, panting, Beth spread the blanket on the ground. "Wonder what happened to the dog?"

"I see him nosing around in the bushes—probably scented a rabbit."

"And he wouldn't know what to do with one if he caught it."

Their lunch consisted of ham-salad sandwiches, apples, slices of chocolate cake, and a container of iced tea. They ate slowly, and in silence, until Clark spoke, "Now, what else do you think needs to be done to the house?"

"What do you have in mind?"

"I'll tear down most of those outbuildings, but there are a couple of log structures that I'll reroof and keep repaired. I'm intending to live here when I'm in the area instead of going to my parents' all the time. I think I'll add an extension to make a new kitchen and bathroom, use the present kitchen as a bedroom, retain the bedroom where you slept, and turn the living area and your parents' bedroom into one large room. I'm going to break through the present ceiling there and open it up to the rafters, to give the room a cathedral ceiling. I'll uncover the old stone fireplace that's been covered with brick. Oh, and add central heat.''

"That sounds great. You might want to add some windows—the house was always so dark."

"I'll put windows in on one whole side of the kitchen to provide a view up this hollow, and a big bay window and two side windows in the living room. I thought I'd have polished oak floors with area rugs, and redo the woodwork to match."

Beth hardly knew how to react when she heard all these plans. She knew without a doubt that Clark was preparing this house for her—for their life together once they'd married. But she had warned him that she couldn't stay in Harlan County. What else could she do?

"This isn't a good location for a home," she said in response. "I think you're renovating a place you can't use much of the time. Even in the summer, the roads are slick when it rains, and even if you grade and limestone them, climbing these two hills becomes almost impossible in the wintertime. You know that."

He grinned. "Of course, as long as I work the way I do, this house would only be a weekend retreat, or a place to live when I'm working in this area. But Shriver Mining equipment could make a nice road down here."

When they'd walked back down the hill, Beth said, "I think I'll go up to the cemetery for a few minutes."

"Do you want me to go along?"

She squeezed his hand. "No, there are some things that I have to face alone."

As a child Beth had played around the cemetery stones, except in the summer, when her mother had always warned, "There're apt to be rattlers in the cemetery now—stay away from it." Beth only needed one such warning.

Even now, she knew that snakes could be crawling in the area, and she watched every step she took, but the small enclosure was relatively free of weeds and brush, and she made her way to her parents' graves in safety. She was sure that Clark had mown the weeds.

John Warner was buried between his two wives. There was a joint tombstone for John and his first wife, but nothing for her mother except a small marker.

Beth knelt by the graves for a few minutes before she went to the lilac bush and broke off some fragrant branches and laid them on her parents' graves. Beth was dry-eyed, but her heart was weeping.

She understood now, that she had wasted most of her teen years wishing for things that she didn't have, instead of being content with what she possessed. She could have made her parents' lives much happier if she had been more cheerful. Her steps were slow as she walked down the hill to where Clark leaned against the vehicle, waiting for her. He put an arm around Beth and drew her close to him.

"I'll have to arrange for a headstone for my mother's grave," she said. "Since you own the property, I suppose I have your permission to send someone to do that."

"You order a stone, and I'll set it for you to save you that expense."

"Thanks."

He opened the door for her, and she noticed that Ranger was already secured in the back, his big frame sprawled out, resting. Earlier Clark had given him plenty of water.

"I've learned some things about myself today, Clark," she said, as they drove away from the house. "I shouldn't have been so dissatisfied. I can see now that my lot wasn't any worse than many other people's around here. I wasted a lot of time feeling sorry for myself when I should have been doing something constructive. It's too bad we can't undo the mistakes of the past."

He took a hand from the steering wheel long enough to pat her on the shoulder. "Don't be too hard on yourself, Bethie. A degree of dissatisfaction can be a good thing. If you'd been contented with your life the way it was, you wouldn't have made an effort to graduate from high school or have gone on to nursing school." He smiled at her, and chucked her under the chin. "And look on the *really* bright side—if you hadn't persevered and gone to high school, you might never have met *me*."

"You're joking, of course, but I do appreciate you very much, Clark."

Getting serious, he said, "My lips were joking, but my heart wasn't. I should have said, 'If you hadn't gone to high school I might not have met *you*.' That would have been a disaster for me, Bethie."

Beth didn't know how to reply. His words had

touched her heart and she felt the same way about him—but didn't dare admit it. She squeezed his hand for a moment and stared out her window to hide her tear-glazed eyes.

The spring rains had started, and almost every day for a week, the river behind the clinic overflowed its banks. The ground was saturated, and the word *flood* was prominent in every conversation Beth heard at the clinic. After work, when Beth took Ranger for his daily walk, she had to clean the mud off the dog before he could be admitted to the house.

One afternoon, Dr. Andrews couldn't keep his schedule because the road between Harlan and the clinic was closed, but it didn't matter since most of her patients were marooned in their homes by the rising river and creeks. And still the weather forecast called for heavy rain.

It was frightening for Beth to realize that she was practically living on an island. Clark's voice was especially welcome when he telephoned from Lexington.

"How are you?"

"Stranded, high and dry, so far," Beth answered with a laugh. "I can't get out, and no one can get in."

"You're safe enough because the clinic is on that hill, but I don't like you to be alone."

"What could harm me?"

"You might get sick."

"Remember, I'm a nurse. I can take care of myself."

"Nevertheless, I'm coming down. I'll bring one of

the company's service trucks with high axles and wheels, so I can drive through the water. And I want to check on the folks, too—I can't get them on the phone."

"The phone service is out in a lot of areas. But don't take chances by driving through high water, Clark—the police are warning against that. We'll be all right."

"No, Beth. I'll be happier if I check out the situation myself. See you in a few hours."

Thunder and lightning heralded the coming of more rain, and soon it sounded as if the clouds had opened up and dumped all of their water at once. The rainfall was so heavy that Beth couldn't see more than a few feet from the house. Then the skies exploded into a splay of light that looked like a fireworks show on Independence Day, a terrific clap of thunder shook the house, and the picture window cracked from top to bottom.

"Oh!" Beth screamed and jumped back from the window, fearing a spray of glass, but the window remained in its frame. Cowering behind the sofa, she saw another flash of lightning across the sky, then heard a tree crash to the ground. It must have been one of the huge oaks on the riverbank, but the downpour was so heavy she couldn't see. Whining, Ranger came to her side, and she put her arm around his quivering shoulders.

It was dark inside the building, and Beth stood and turned on the lights, but soon they flickered and the power went off. Beth had a flashlight ready for such a situation. She searched in her closet and found a battery radio, and huddling in the bedroom with Ranger beside her, she tuned into a local station. The soft music was soothing, and she relaxed a little, but then she sat up, rigid with fright, when the radio announcer suddenly spoke.

"We interrupt this program to bring you the latest flood news. Eastern Kentucky is being deluged with torrential thunderstorms. The Army Corps of Engineers in both Harlan and Pineville have issued orders for the closing of the floodgates, although any prediction on the expected crest of the waters can't be made until the rains stop. At present, there is no indication when the rain will cease."

He paused and the music he had interrupted continued soft and serene. It seemed to Beth that the rain had lessened somewhat, and she looked at her wristwatch in the dim light. Almost five o'clock. How long would it take Clark to arrive? Or could he even get through the waters now? If they were closing the floodgates in Harlan, he couldn't drive the regular route.

Her heart ached with fear for him, and visions of cars and trucks washed away in floodwaters raced through her head. She prayed that he'd do the sensible thing and turn back, but somehow she knew he wouldn't.

The music stopped again. "This late-breaking news has just been received at the station. According to the weather bureau, a series of cloudbursts has occurred in the Daniel Boone National Forest, and residents living in hollows and low-lying valleys adjacent to the forests are warned to evacuate to higher ground. The area, sometimes called Raccoon Creek by the locals, already deluged by flooding early this morning, is targeted for another onslaught of water. Heed this warning. At the first indication of flooding, seek higher ground. Do *not* stay in your homes.''

When the lights flickered and came on again, Beth sighed deeply. She shut off the flashlight and turned on the TV. She found the local news station, but she didn't learn as much from the Lexington television station as she had on the radio. Fearing that the picture window might fall from the frame, she brought heavy tape from the clinic and taped over the cracks.

The downpour worsened before she heard a vehicle and peered out to see a monstrous truck driving up to her back door. She held the door open as Clark jumped from the truck and came running. He was dripping wet and looked terrified, and for once, he ignored Ranger's joyous welcome.

''Did you have much trouble getting here?''

''It was slow driving because I had to take a lot of detours. But, Beth, did you hear that radio announcement about Raccoon Creek? That's where my family lives.''

''Oh, Clark! I thought the name sounded familiar.''

''That's not its real name, but it's what the residents call it. No wonder I couldn't get Mother on the phone—it sounds like everything has been washed away.''

''Surely it isn't that bad! What are you going to do?''

''Go and find out what has happened to them.''

"How can you? The water is everywhere. It's too high to drive there safely."

"I can't drive, not even with the big truck—there's probably six feet of water in the way—but I can walk back through the mountains."

Glancing out the window where the rain was pouring down and the yard looked like a lake, while lightning still quivered across the sky and thunder sounded in the distance, Beth said, "It will be dark in an hour."

"I can't help that. I have to go." Clark was pacing back and forth in the kitchen, with Ranger following his steps, anxiously peering up into his face. The dog wasn't used to being ignored by Clark.

"Then I'm going with you," Beth said.

"No—I can't risk that. I'll have to walk at least ten miles, and I might not be able to get through. If I've lost my family already, I won't take a chance on losing you."

Beth took his arm and pushed him into a chair. "Clark, listen to me. You're not being rational."

"But you don't know what a flood in one of those narrow hollows can be like. I've seen more than one valley completely cleared by the surging waters. I have to try to reach them anyway."

She knelt beside him. "I can understand that, but calm down before you make decisions. What should we take with us?"

"Beth, you can't go. It's too hard a trip."

She took his hands and held them tightly. "Clark, if the situation was reversed and my parents were marooned and in danger, would you go with me?"

"Of course, but that would be different."

"I'm not letting you go alone. Your father is too wise to be caught napping in a situation like this, and I'm sure they are safe, *but* if you should happen on a tragedy, I want to be with you. Can't you understand that?"

He reached out his arms and drew her close. "All right, Bethie, I do understand. Let's get started."

"I know I'll delay you, but I want to go with you. Besides, a nurse might be useful. I'll take a backpack of medical supplies. I have two packs that I used in school—do you want to carry the other one?"

"We can't take much, for we can't be weighted down. Actually, I'm intending to follow an abandoned railroad track most of the way, so the going may not be too rough."

While Beth went into the clinic to fill her pack with bandages and medicines, Clark checked the truck where he found two battery-operated lanterns, and a large thermos bottle. "I'll make some coffee and fill the thermos, and I'll get food from your cabinets and refrigerator and put it in your other backpack. We don't know what we'll run into."

After Beth selected all the basic medications she thought she might need, she had a bit of space left in the backpack, and feeling a bit foolish she dropped in a fetoscope and some of the other instruments she needed for a birth. *Once a midwife, always a midwife,* she derided herself.

Clark was just tightening the top on the thermos when she returned to the kitchen.

"You didn't have much food to choose from," he

said. "You should always lay in a supply of groceries when there are flood warnings."

"I didn't think about it. What kind of clothes should I wear?" she asked, eyeing his jeans, heavy woolen shirt, and thick-soled leather boots.

"I have another long slicker in the truck, and you should have rain gear of some kind. Also, put on the heaviest boots you have and warm clothes. It's going to be cold in the mountains tonight, and even with raincoats, we're going to be wet."

Before she went off to dress, Beth encouraged Clark to have a snack and a warm drink. There was no telling when he'd last eaten and they would certainly need their energy for the long hike.

Fortunately, Beth had needed wool-lined boots during her stay in Pennsylvania, and she found them in the back of her closet. She pulled on a pair of heavy socks and stuck a spare in her knapsack. She selected a soft cotton turtleneck to wear under a plaid wool sweater that she only used in the coldest weather. She started to put on jeans, but decided that her corduroy slacks were warmer.

After she'd dressed, she joined Clark in the kitchen. "What about Ranger?" she asked as she hurriedly ate a few crackers with peanut butter at the kitchen counter.

"I'm putting him outside in the barn. We may be gone for several days. I'll put him on a long leash with plenty of food and water, and leave the door open. He'll be all right."

Before they left the house, Clark clasped Beth's hands in his. "I've been so busy in my preparations that I forgot to do the most important thing. Let's have a word of prayer.''

Beth freed her hands and put both arms around Clark. He leaned his head on her hair.

"God, still my troubled heart," he prayed. "Thank you for Beth, who said the right words to calm me. Care for us tonight, as well as for my other loved ones. Whatever the outcome, we still love You, Lord." He lifted his head, his eyes glistening with tears. Beth wiped them away and he leaned to kiss her tenderly, and pulled the hood of her raincoat over her head.

"Ready?"

She smiled at him, as if to prove she didn't fear what was before them, but she was sure that Clark had noticed her trembling knees. If she could hardly stand now, how could she walk ten miles tonight?

"Ready."

Clark locked the door to the building and hid the key in his truck. Ranger barked mournfully from the barn, and Beth had to steel herself against his misery. Clark bypassed the truck and headed up the valley. They walked side by side for a mile, but they didn't talk, for the wind-driven rain pelted their faces. The moisture found the open place above the collar of Beth's coat, and she felt water running down the front of her sweater. Much more of this, and they would both be drenched.

They heard the angry, tumultuous river long before they reached it, and when they neared the small bridge where Clark had expected to cross, both approaches were submerged in the muddy water, and the white-capped current lapped at the bottom of the bridge.

"Well, that's out," Clark said bleakly. "We can't cross here." He pointed downstream to the railroad bridge. "Think you can walk across that?"

Cross that high, narrow structure without any rails to cling to?

She turned startled eyes to Clark—surely he was joking! But his face was serious.

"If you think it's safe, I'll try." She didn't want to make the trip any harder for him by refusing to go forward now. She knew he must be terribly worried about his family.

"Let's go see. We have to get across the river before dark."

The water was still rising, and the waves lapped at their feet as they hurried away toward higher ground to gain access to the railroad bridge. It wasn't a long bridge because the river was narrow at this point, but when Beth, following Clark, stepped out onto the railway ties and looked down at the murky torrent swirling a few feet below her, she gasped and retreated.

"Go on back home, Beth. This is too dangerous for you to try."

She clamped her lips together in determination. "I'm going, Clark, one way or another. You may need me. You go first, and I'll follow."

Looking doubtful, Clark walked slowly forward on the structure. Halfway across, he turned and saw that she wasn't following.

"Afraid, Beth?"

She nodded, and he turned around. "I'll come back and lead you across. I should have thought of that, but I haven't been thinking as well as I should."

"No, you go on, Clark!" she shouted, for it was difficult to hear above the roaring river. "If I panic, I might pull you down. Let me try it once more."

Swallowing with difficulty, Beth closed her eyes and stepped out onto the bridge. As long as she didn't see the swirling water, she would be all right, but obviously she couldn't cross the bridge with her eyes shut. She inched forward about a foot, and her head swam dizzily.

God, I have to get across this river. I can't let Clark face this situation by himself.

But she was still dizzy, and she called to Clark, who was almost on the other side. "I'm going to crawl across—I just can't walk."

"Beth, why don't you go back home? I'd understand."

She shook her head, shifted her backpack a little higher, and gingerly knelt on the bridge. She would have to be careful that she didn't get her feet caught in the wide cracks. Carefully, inch by inch, Beth crawled across the bridge, calmly enough, except when an uprooted tree rammed against one of the supports and the bridge shuddered. It seemed like hours, but in reality it was only ten minutes before Beth reached the other side, and gratefully took Clark's waiting hand to help her to stand. Her knees burned, her gloves were soaked, and her legs trembled, but she gave him a quivery smile.

"I hope we don't have to cross any more bridges like this—that experience was enough to last me a lifetime."

For the first time since he'd arrived at the clinic,

Clark grinned slightly. "When all of this is behind us, Bethie, you ask me why I love you so much, and I'll have more reasons to give you." He patted her cheek, where raindrops were sparkling in the lantern's light.

She smiled into his loving eyes and her heart felt suddenly light again. "I keep hoping the rain will stop. What if we run into more creeks?" she asked in a breathless voice.

"This railroad winds along the side of the mountain, and we won't come to any more streams—maybe just a short trestle or two across a hollow. It's a long way to go, but we should make it. We must walk single file, because this track isn't kept clear anymore, and the forest and underbrush are moving across it in spots. You follow, and let me know if you need to stop. I want to travel fast as long as we have a little daylight."

Lowering her head against the driving rain, Beth plodded along the rails, watching her steps carefully, for in places the track was perched on the mountainside with nothing to break a fall if she should stumble. When the darkness intensified, Clark paused and handed her one of the lanterns he carried.

"Tired?" he asked.

"Very."

"I am, too. We'll stop in another mile or so and eat a snack. I've been looking for a shelter of some kind to get out of the rain."

She nodded wearily, wondering if she could possibly walk any farther, but with each step Clark moved forward, she trudged after him. The rain was uncomfortable, but Beth was more concerned about the light-

ning, because it was sometimes bright enough to il-
luminate the whole sky. At other times, the flashes
came almost to the ground, and she screamed when a
brilliant bolt struck with a deafening sound only a few
feet ahead of them, and she heard shattering wood.

Clark dropped his lantern and ran toward her. "Get
down, Beth!" he shouted, and when he reached her,
he pushed her to the ground and covered her with his
body. Another streak of lightning illuminated the sky,
and they saw a huge tree on the mountainside above
the track sway precariously. With a shudder and a
deafening sound of cracking wood, the tree toppled to
the ground, completely blocking their path. The
branches of the tree spread over them.

For a few moments there was absolute quiet around
them; even the rain stopped. The only sound Beth
could hear was the thumping of her heart, and it clam-
ored as loud as a freight train in her ears.

"That was close, Beth. Are you hurt?"

"I don't think so. I'm not hurting anywhere."

"Let's see if we can crawl out from under these
branches. Luckily the trunk didn't split completely, so
it's held most of the weight of the limbs off us." He
moved away from Beth, pulled the limbs back for her
to follow him, then took the battery lantern from her.
With the other hand, he helped her to stand.

He flashed the light ahead of him. "I dropped my
lantern—it's underneath that tree trunk. We'll have to
make do with one light from now on."

Beth shivered when she thought of how close they'd
come to being trapped or injured by that massive
trunk.

"We'll start up the mountain, for we can't climb over this."

"Clark, I don't think I can go any farther. I'm sorry—I should have stayed behind like you wanted me to."

He took a few steps up the incline and held out a hand to her. "Come on, Bethie. This isn't a hard climb. I'll help you."

Beth gritted her teeth in grim determination. He had always been there for her when she needed him, and now that she was presented with this one opportunity to help him, she had to go on. She moved to follow him but slipped in the mud, and as she slid backward, she dropped to her knees, stifling a scream. She must have skinned her knees more than she'd thought when she'd crawled across the bridge. Any pressure on her knees was agonizing, but spurred on by Clark's gentle tugging on her hand and his constant encouragement, she managed to claw her way up.

When they reached the spot from which the large tree had toppled, they passed around the upended root system and started down toward the railroad right of way again. "We have to stay near those tracks," Clark said, "or I'll get lost. Let's find them again, and then we'll sit down and rest."

But the wet, rocky soil crumbled beneath them making their feet fly out from under them, and they slid forward rapidly on their posteriors. "Well, at least we found the tracks," Clark grunted, when his leg hit one of the steel rails. Flashing his light around them, he said, "We're in luck—there's a little shelter a few feet away, probably used by the railroad to store repair parts for the tracks.''

Water leaked through the roof of the shack, but Beth sank down on the wet floor, happy to be off her feet under any conditions. After a quick look at his watch, Clark turned off the light. ''We'll have to save the battery—we would really be in trouble if we had no light.''

''What time is it?''

''It's midnight. I wish I knew how close we are. I want to rush on as fast as possible, for I'm uneasy, but I know we have to conserve our strength.''

As tired as she was, Beth still feared they would find the worst and then, at least, she could be a comfort to Clark. She couldn't do much comforting when she was cowering on the ground, concerned over her own discomfort.

''Sit here beside me, Clark. A few minutes of rest won't delay us that much, or change the situation your folks are in.'' She patted the wet floor, and he sat down heavily beside her. She put her arms around him.

''Your family will be all right, sweetheart. You know how capable and practical your mother is.''

''But Daddy is so lame—he couldn't move very fast if they had to climb the mountain.''

''Anna would have looked out for him—she's been doing that for a long time. Besides, they've lived on that creek for years and know the dangers. Your dad wouldn't wait until the last minute to leave. And according to the reporter, this cloudburst occurred early in the day. It was probably still daylight when the worst came. They wouldn't have been taken by surprise.''

''I've been hoping that they could have reached a barn that's up on the mountain. It's about a mile from the house, but if they got there, they will be safe and have shelter, even though it won't be comfortable for them.''

''I'm sure that's where they are. Turn around and I'll get the thermos from your backpack so we can have coffee and some food. What did you pack, anyway?''

''Crackers, cheese, and granola bars. I picked up a few bananas, too, but they may have been mashed when that tree fell on us. You didn't have much in stock,'' he reminded accusingly, and Beth laughed.

''You've already told me that. As you know, I don't worry much about eating.''

Fumbling in the dark, she unzipped the backpack and handed him the thermos. ''We'll have to drink out of the same cup—you didn't put in an extra. Let's eat a banana each and a granola bar, and save the rest until later.''

After they'd eaten, Beth drew Clark's head down on her shoulder. ''Nap a little, if you can.'' When he didn't protest, Beth wondered if Clark had ever had much coddling. No doubt, most of Anna's time had been taken up with her handicapped husband and the two girls, leaving Clark to fend for himself. Tenderly, Beth wiped the rain from his face with her handkerchief and smoothed back his damp hair. He had such a handsome face, she never tired of looking at him. Lowly, she sang a few verses of a song that she'd heard often in Abner's church. The lyrics praised God's unfailing love and care.

"I didn't know you could sing, Beth," he said softly when she had finished.

"That's because you sing so loudly in church, you can't hear me." She felt his facial muscles relaxing in a grin against her shoulder. "Besides, I'm not much of a singer. I'll never be invited to Carnegie Hall, but I can carry a tune."

"The congregation sang that song last Sunday, and I can still hear Daddy bellowing out the lyrics. You're right to remind me of God's ever-abiding care. I've been acting like a child, and it's a wonder God hasn't shouted to me, 'O ye of little faith.'"

"Take a few minutes to relax, Clark." Beth caressed the wet skin below his cap and softly kissed the beard-roughened cheek nearest her mouth. She believed he did nap a bit, for it must have been fifteen minutes before he stirred.

"It's tempting to stay here, but we'd better move." He stood stiffly and pulled Beth upward. "You'll never know how much I appreciate your company tonight, Bethie. Thanks for making me bring you."

"There's no place else I'd rather be." Beth knew that tonight marked a new dimension in her relationship with Clark. Always, before, he had treated her like a china doll to be treasured and coddled, displayed on a pedestal. He was continually shielding her, trying to bear the brunt of any problems she faced, and watching for every opportunity to make life easier for her. Sometimes she believed that he still considered her the teenage girl he had first loved, rather than a woman who could share his trouble, sorrow, and joy. After tonight, she knew he would regard her in a different light.

Mile after mile Beth plodded after Clark, stumbling often, because she had scant light from the lantern he carried. She dulled her mind to what she endured in the next few hours. She reasoned that if she didn't think, she wouldn't feel the pain in her feet where the wet boots and soggy socks had rubbed blisters, or shiver with the chills that coursed up and down her spine due to the damp pants that clung to her legs, or inhale the woolly smell of her sweater, soaked where the rain had gotten under her raincoat.

The trestles frightened her the most, but after she had crawled across the second one, fearful that she would plunge into the deep ravine along which a torrent of water was rushing, she was no longer afraid of them. A few times, their journey was eased when the rain stopped, and the moon popped out from behind the dark clouds. Clark paused occasionally to rest, and just when Beth thought that she couldn't take another step, he looked at his watch.

"It's four o'clock, and I think we're almost home. I've hunted in the woods back of our house, and if I can find a certain black walnut, I'll know where I am."

"Pretty hard to find a particular tree now, isn't it?"

"Not the one I'm looking for—it's the biggest black walnut anyone around here has ever seen. You sit on this rock and rest a minute while I look around."

"Don't get lost, Clark. I'd never find my way out of here."

She heard his tired steps dragging into the forest, and it seemed a long time before he returned. "I found it, Beth!" he said in an excited voice, his fatigue forgotten now that he felt their goal was within reach. "We have only another mile to go and it's all downhill."

Beth tried to stand, but her right leg buckled with a painful cramp. She fell to her knees—knees that were bruised, raw and bleeding. She clamped her jaws together to hold back a groan, for she didn't want Clark to know her condition. He helped her to stand again and held her arm until she said, "I'm all right now. It was a muscle cramp."

When they came out of the forest at last, Clark pointed ahead. "That's the barn down there—you can see it in the moonlight. I'm afraid to call out, Beth. What if they aren't there?"

"That won't mean they aren't safe somewhere else. I'll go on alone and look for them if you want me to."

"You must think I'm an awful coward, Beth, but when I thought my whole family might have perished, I just lost control."

"I could never think you're a coward, not after you came to my parents' funeral so many years ago—one Randolph among a whole family of Warners. You earned my respect then, Clark, and everything you've done since has only raised my estimation of you."

"I guess you do know how I feel now, Beth, since you lost both your parents at one time."

"And it's something I don't want to happen to you."

Taking a deep breath, Clark yelled, "Daddy!

Mother! Where are you?'' He seemed to be holding his breath. "Daddy!'' he yelled again.

Clark grabbed Beth's arm. "Look! I see a light in the barn. They've heard us.'' A sob escaped his lips when Abner Randolph answered, "Is that you, son? We're all safe here in the barn.''

Clark dropped to his knees, and Beth cuddled his head against her body as he whispered, "Thank You, God. Oh, thank You for your mercy.''

Abner was standing outside the barn now, flashing a light in their direction. "Come on down, Clark.''

Beth was weak with relief now that they had arrived safely at their destination to find the Randolphs were all right. Clark's shoulders sagged with relief and his steps, too, slowed as he and Beth picked their way gingerly toward the barn. The roar of water plunging down the hollow indicated that the creek was still raging, and she wondered if there was any residence left in the area, or if the water had made a clean sweep.

Abner, Anna and their two girls were standing in the barn opening when Clark and Beth stumbled and slid down the last bank.

"Who's that you've got with you, Clark?'' Anna asked.

"How in the world did you get to us?'' Abner wondered aloud.

"We walked around the mountain on that abandoned railroad bed.''

"Why, it's Beth, Mother,'' Sallie said.

Clark threw his arms around his parents. "I feared I'd lost all of you. When I heard that Raccoon Creek was on a rampage, I thought you might have been caught in the flood. I had to find out, but the roads are all blocked."

"Come in out of the wet where it's more comfortable," Anna said. "When did the two of you start?"

"About six o'clock last evening," Beth said as she eased down on a pile of hay. "Oh," she whispered, "An inner-spring mattress never felt so good."

"You shouldn't have brought her, Clark," Anna said with concern. She knelt beside Beth and started to unlace her boots. Beth had made an attempt, but her fingers were numb with cold.

"Now don't blame me for that," Clark said, the tone of his voice light and jovial now. "She's a stubborn female. She was determined to come."

"I wasn't going to let him come alone, when we didn't know how you were."

Anna lifted her head. She didn't say anything, but Beth could see the gratitude in her eyes, her gratitude that Beth had taken care of her son.

"If the cloudburst had come at night, we might not have gotten out," Abner said, "but I've seen storms at the head of this hollow before. When it kept raining, Anna and I decided we'd come up here. If there wasn't a flood, all it would cost us would have been a long walk."

"It was terrible, Clark," Mary Lynn said. "We hadn't been up here five minutes, when a wall of water gushed down the valley."

"The water had been rising rapidly for the past twenty-four hours, and there wasn't any place for all of it to spread out," Abner said. "I've never seen anything like it—reminded me of the way God made a wall out of the waters of the Red Sea and let the Israelites march across.''

"What about your home?" Beth asked.

"We haven't seen anything since it got dark," Sallie replied, and her eyes filled with tears. "But there was about ten feet of water where the house stood the last we saw—nothing visible except the television antenna."

"Did you save anything?" Clark asked anxiously.

"Only the clothes we have on and a few blankets," Abner said, "but we brought two sacks of foodstuffs, and several jugs of water. It's hard to believe that a lifetime of savings could be wiped out in an hour."

"I don't suppose you know about the neighbors on up the hollow?" Clark asked.

"Yes, we do," Abner told him. "The girls walked around the mountain before dark, and we think everyone is safe. But, of course, the houses are gone, probably all of the livestock, too."

"I guess we had our long walk for nothing, Clark," Beth said. "I brought along medical supplies, but I'm pleased they won't be needed." She could hardly keep her eyes open. She felt as if she could sleep for hours.

"I don't know about that," Anna warned. "I hesitate to mention this, but our neighbor, Cheryl Carmichael, told Sallie that she thought she was starting labor pains. I intended to go as soon as it got daylight, but you probably would be more help."

"Cheryl is one of my patients. She's been coming to me for examinations, and I intended to go to her home to deliver her child. But she isn't due for another month, if I remember."

"That's right," Anna said. "But trying to save her family from the flood must have been a strain on her and started her pains early."

"Is she alone?"

"Her husband and two children. I hated to tell you when you're so tired, but she may need help."

"I'll go, of course, and do what I can." Beth had thought twice about putting maternity necessities in her backpack, unsure if she'd need them, but now she realized it was a good thing.

"Maybe you should wait until daylight," Sallie suggested.

"If she was starting labor pains before dark, I need to go now, if one of you will show me the way," Beth said wearily, as she struggled to her feet.

"I'll go," Sallie offered.

"No," Clark said decisively. "I'm going. Do you know where the Carmichaels found shelter?"

"In that old shed where they used to keep their goats," Mary Lynn interjected. "It's not very clean."

"You can take these blankets," Anna said. "Clark, you come back for me if I'm needed."

Chapter Eight

The rain started again as they left the barn, but the path was easy to follow and wide enough that they could walk side by side.

"The Carmichaels are our nearest neighbors, so we only have to walk about a half mile. Think you can make it?" Clark asked her.

"I'll have to. I was thinking of my Granny Warner, and I surely have more respect for her than I used to. She wandered over these mountains and valleys on foot and horseback *all* of the time when she was a midwife. So, I shouldn't mind a little bit of discomfort."

Clark put his arm around her shoulders, and although it hampered her stride, it was comforting to know that strong arm was there for her protection. They had drunk some coffee before they left the Randolphs, and they nibbled on cheese and crackers as they limped along the trail. By the time they reached the Carmichael property, it was light enough that they could see without the lantern. Sam Carmichael saw them coming, and he stepped into view.

"Down here. We're in the shack!" he called. "Well, hello, Clark, and is this Miss Warner with you? Were you down at Abner's when the water struck?"

"No, we walked over the mountain last night. I couldn't get in touch with my family, and I was worried."

"Well, I'm mighty glad to see you. Cheryl's time has come," Sam said.

"Yes, Mrs. Randolph told me," Beth said. "I'll see if I can help her."

But her heart sank when she saw the tiny shack where the Carmichaels had taken shelter. Cheryl was lying on the dirt floor with only a blanket under her. Her two little girls were sitting beside her, wide-eyed and scared.

"Hello, Miss Warner," Cheryl said, and cringed as a tremor of pain surged through her body. "Our birthing plans didn't include this, did they?"

"No, but we'll manage. Fortunately, I brought some of my equipment along. I'll give you a quick exam and see how much longer you have to wait. Have you been timing your contractions?"

"Not very well. We didn't bring a clock with us. We were lucky to get out of the house with our lives. But judging from how I felt with my other two, I don't think it will be long. The cramps are getting much worse."

As Beth lifted her dress, Cheryl asked, "Should the little ones leave?"

"Not as far as I'm concerned. And your husband

and Clark should come inside, also. It's raining hard again."

"Sam has never been at any of my deliveries."

Beth monitored the baby with her fetoscope, and after checking Cheryl's progress as well as she could, she said, "It's high time he attends one, then. I'll call the men, if you won't be too embarrassed. Let's make this a true family affair. You aren't going to have long to wait anyway."

Beth joined the men, who were looking over the vast destruction before them. The water had dropped rapidly, and the Carmichael mobile home was ruined. It had been washed off its foundation and wrapped around a tree. Their car was suspended in the limbs of a maple tree.

"Come on inside. The baby will be born before long."

"Oh, I wouldn't want to do that," Sam said. "It might make Cheryl uncomfortable."

Beth laughed at him. "You mean it might make *you* uncomfortable, Sam. Don't be afraid. I may need some help."

When Sam hesitated, Clark said, "I'll help you, Beth." *How many times since she'd known him, had he said, "I'll help you, Beth?"* He stooped to enter the low-ceiling structure and spoke to Cheryl.

"I don't want her lying on the ground," Beth told him. "Help me as I walk with her, and if Sam won't come in, you can support her when the child is ready to be born."

Sam eventually came into the shack, looking as if he would bolt if anyone looked at him. "Sam, you stand where Clark is and support her shoulders. Clark, you might open that bottle of water I brought and try to find something soft and relatively clean to wrap the baby in later.''

It wasn't long before Cheryl's son was born, and Beth used a soft cloth she'd brought in her backpack and bottled water to clean the baby as best she could. She wrapped him in a sweatshirt donated by one of the younger girls, then gave him into the arms of his father. Beth had never seen a prouder man, and the two girls crowded around their parents to see their new brother.

To place a newborn in its mother's arms was always a tender moment for Beth and it was even more rewarding when the whole family was present for the birth, rejoicing over the new baby. This had to be joy at its highest. Would such pleasure ever come her way?

As Beth knelt beside the Carmichaels and silently celebrated with them, she compared Cheryl's radiance now to her agony of the past few hours. What would it be like to bear a child of her own and to know the love of a husband such as Sam displayed when, with his son still cradled in his left arm, he pulled Cheryl close and kissed her so lovingly?

Beth glanced up at Clark, who was also watching the Carmichaels, a yearning expression on his face. He knelt beside her and drew her into a close embrace. She leaned against Clark, drawing strength from his sturdy body and placed her head on his shoulder. If she'd marry Clark, they could share the same joy the

Carmichaels knew. No doubt, Clark was thinking the same thing.

After Beth made Cheryl as comfortable as was possible under such conditions, she and Clark prepared to leave. "Is there any chance of getting out of here, Clark?" Sam asked. "Cheryl can't stay up here with the children."

Clark shook his head in concern. "I don't know how to answer. There are no doubt lots of bridges and roads washed out between here and Harlan, so even when the water recedes, it will be a long time before you can get out. I imagine the National Guard will be dropping supplies to everyone. After I rest some, I'll walk back to Harlan and let people know how you are, and I'll come back to help as soon as I possibly can."

Beth was almost asleep on her feet when she reached the Randolphs' barn, and she sank down on the pile of hay that had been so inviting before. She had been out of bed for more than thirty-six hours, and ten hours of that time, she'd been climbing over terrain that a goat would have had trouble negotiating. No wonder she was tired. She didn't even know when Anna removed her boots and socks and spread a blanket over her.

When Beth awakened, she was alone in the barn. She went outside and looked down the mountain and could have cried at the ruined home below her. She remembered how clean and neat it had been when she'd visited the Randolphs, and thought particularly of the wall that Anna had covered with pictures of her three children. Now all of that was gone.

She could see the Randolphs working around their

home, and with difficulty, she walked down to be with them. Every joint in her body was stiff and sore. Her clothes were filthy and still damp from their trek last night. When she could get clean clothes, she didn't know, but that seemed a minor problem compared to those of Clark's sisters, who wouldn't have any clothing.

Beth waded in mud and slime that rose above her boot tops as she moved toward the house, and the insides of her boots were soon as dirty as the outside. The doors were wide-open, and Clark and his sisters were using brooms to push the mud from the house as the water receded. Abner sat on the porch in a straight chair watching them.

"The water must have dropped in a hurry," she said to Abner.

He nodded. "When it got dark last night, only the television antenna was sticking above the water. Now there's only a few feet, as you can see."

When Clark heard her talking, he said, "The house has withstood the flooding better than we had hoped. Almost everything inside was either washed away or ruined by the water, but the house still stands. Mother's in the kitchen seeing if she can salvage anything."

"But if you hadn't bricked the building a few years ago, it would have washed away," Abner said.

Sallie and Mary Lynn were both crying as they shoveled out mud and water, and Beth's own eyes filled with tears. How terrible it must be to lose everything!

"What can I do to help?"

"Maybe you could find a good beefsteak and cook it for us. We're getting hungry." Abner grinned at Beth, but she knew it was no joking matter. There wasn't any food except what they had carried up to the barn the day before.

"Here, Mary Lynn, let me spell you on that broom for a while," Beth said, and she took the broom from the girl's hand.

"What are we going to do for food?" Sallie asked.

"I figure the National Guard helicopters will fly over today and drop some provisions," Clark said. "I intend to leave tomorrow and walk back over the mountain. I'll have to notify Milton where I am, and I'm sure he'll put all of the mine equipment at the disposal of the residents who've lost so much. I imagine there are many other areas that are flooded."

"Could the mine have been damaged, too?" Beth asked.

"Not likely—the land is high there, but the roads into it will be closed."

The water was squishing in Beth's boots, her hands were rough and red, and her head hurt from lack of sleep. She had never been so uncomfortable, and she thought longingly of her apartment. "Should I go with you?"

"I've been wondering about that. I'll travel in daylight, and the trip will be easier. In fact, I'm wondering about taking Mary Lynn and Sallie, too."

Anna appeared in the kitchen doorway, holding a plastic dishpan. It was covered with mud, but probably still usable. "I wish you would take them, Clark.

We'll leave as soon as we can find transportation for Abner.''

''But where will you go?'' Beth asked.

''We own a little house in Harlan that we rent, and it happens to be vacant right now. We'll live there until we can rebuild here.''

''That's where we lived when I went to school in Harlan,'' Clark said. ''Remember?''

Late that evening, a helicopter did appear over Raccoon Creek, and dropped a bag of supplies. It contained some food, a gallon of water, and some blankets.

''If you girls are game, we'll leave in the morning for Harlan,'' Clark said after they investigated the bag. ''With what you saved from the house, there will be enough food here to last Daddy and Mother for a few days, and by that time, I think we can fix the roads so Daddy can be taken out of the hollow.''

''Mary Lynn and Sallie can stay with me until that time,'' Beth offered.

''I'd appreciate that, Beth,'' Anna replied. ''It will take us a while to find furniture for the house.''

''If we're going to leave in the morning, I should go back to Carmichaels' and see how Cheryl and the baby are getting along,'' Beth said.

''I'll walk along with you,'' Clark told her.

The rain had finally stopped, and a sunset tinged with pink hues highlighting a vivid blue sky was a pleasant sight as they crippled along, for Clark, too, was feeling the effects of their nightlong journey.

''Beth,'' Clark said, ''you've been such a help to me these past few days. I've never really appreciated you enough, and certainly didn't realize what a blessing your profession is to others. I'd never been present at a birth before, but I was impressed by how easily you handled Cheryl. And even Sam, who was scared to death, was as calm as could be, when he was helping you. As I told you before, you have a gift of service to others. You dealt with that birth as if it were just a common everyday occurrence.''

"Which it really is," Beth said with a laugh. "Women have been bearing children since Eve brought the first baby into the world. I didn't do anything extraordinary.''

"You shouldn't put down your skill that way. I believe that you have more than your share of expertise as a midwife. Whatever it is, I admire you.''

"Thank you, Clark.''

When, by the light of day, Beth saw the trail they'd taken to get to Raccoon Creek, she couldn't believe that they had traveled safely over such terrain when it was pitch-dark and pouring rain. The trestles they had walked—or in her case, crawled across—to pass deep ravines were piddling little structures that seemed too frail to hold their weight.

She had hoped that the water would be low enough that they could cross the river by the bridge rather than the railroad trestle, but her hopes were dashed; the river was even higher than it had been two days ago.

Sallie screamed when she learned she was expected to cross the railroad bridge with the water slopping up between the cross ties, but when, with a sigh, Beth got down on her knees and started crawling across, Clark's two sisters followed her example.

Ranger saw them coming from a mile away, and he bellowed out a joyous welcome. As they entered the house, Beth said, ''Welcome. Shall we draw straws to see who gets first dibs on the bathtub?''

''I'm going to pass up a bath and head back to Lexington as soon as I telephone the company,'' Clark said. ''I wouldn't have any clean clothing here, so I'll shower when I get back to the apartment.''

''Be sure and bring some clothes for us when you come back, Clark,'' Mary Lynn told him.

''Write down your sizes, and I'll do what I can.''

''Sallie, you and Mary Lynn can bathe first,'' Beth told them. ''And I'll try to find you some things to wear. I don't have very many clothes to start with, and my clothes won't fit you, but they'll be clean.''

''You'll have to make do—it will be several days before you can get into Harlan to buy anything,'' Clark warned. ''I don't know what you can do for food.''

''I have some cans of soup we can open, and several frozen dinners. We won't starve,'' Beth said.

''I'll try to return tomorrow with everything you need,'' Clark replied.

By the time he had finished with his call to the office in Lexington, his sisters were taking baths. He stood looking at Beth for a minute, then he grinned. ''I've never seen you look more beautiful.''

She glanced in the mirror, and she hardly recognized herself. Her clothes were ragged and muddy, her face was streaked with mud and tears, and one large scratch ran from her ear down to her throat. Her hair was matted and stringy because she hadn't thought to take a comb with her.

"Everyone to his own opinion," she said lightly. "You look pretty handsome, too. I just hope a policeman won't arrest you as a vagrant."

Clark's appearance was as bad as hers. He had left his boots and socks on the back step, and his bare feet were encrusted with mud.

Clark put his arms around her. "I mean it, Bethie— you've never seemed more beautiful to me. You could have stayed here at the clinic and been warm and safe, yet you risked your life to go with me. You've become the Florence Nightingale that you wanted to be. Even in the Crimea, I'll judge she didn't suffer any worse than you have in the past two days."

She pulled his face down and kissed him on the cheek. "I'm just paying you back for all the good things you've done for me."

"I think we can do better than that," Clark said, and his arms tightened around her until she could hardly breathe. His rough beard scratched her face, but she soon forgot the discomfort as he kissed her. The love she had for him had never been greater, and she was on the verge of saying, "Clark, let's get married right away," but when he released her lips, the words didn't come.

"I love you, Bethie. I'll be back as soon as I can."

Beth and her guests watched the evening news while they ate the meal that she was able to prepare with her few groceries. All three of them were ravenous after their strenuous trek and lack of food, but they knew they had to conserve what they had until Clark returned.

The news wasn't as bad as they had feared. Only Raccoon Creek and one other hollow a few miles away had been totally wiped out, and as far as could be determined, there had been no lives lost. The other rivers and creeks in eastern Kentucky were in flood, also, and emergency shelters were full of those who had been forced from their homes. There was hardly a season that didn't bring flooding somewhere in Kentucky, so Beth had heard all of her life about the misery of flood victims, but she had never before been so closely associated with the disaster.

How she wished she could do something for the Randolphs, who had been so good to her, and her heart ached when she thought of poor Cheryl Carmichael, with three children, one of them a newborn, who had nothing better for a home than a tiny stable. But what could she do? She had no money, and hardly anything else that she could share.

The next morning Beth awakened before Sallie and Mary Lynn. Not wanting to disturb them, she turned on the reading light over her bed and reached for the Bible. The night before, she had thanked God sincerely for keeping His protecting hand over her and Clark as they had wandered through the darkness, and also for the safety of Clark's family.

She reached for the Bible, which opened to the Epistle of James. Beth had already learned that when she had a particular question that needed to be answered from God's Word, the Bible often fell open to the Scripture she needed. Today seemed no exception, as she looked down at the page in front of her.

What good is it, my brothers, if a man claims to have faith but has no deeds? Can such faith save him? Suppose a brother or sister is without clothes and daily food. If one of you says to him, "Go, I wish you well; keep warm and well fed," but does nothing about his physical needs, what good is it? In the same way, faith by itself, if it is not accompanied by action, is dead.

Well, that was plain enough! At times when she read the Bible, Beth failed to understand the meaning or how it applied to her life. What she had just read simply meant that all the sympathy or good wishes in the world wouldn't be of any help to the flood victims. She had to *do* something.

Although she doubted that she would have any patients come to the clinic, Beth had been gone for two days, so she planned to open as usual. Walking as quietly as she could, she dressed, went into the kitchen and drank a glass of milk. Mary Lynn was asleep on a couch in the main office, so Beth closed that door before she went into the examination room.

She telephoned the hospital and asked for Dr. Andrews. "Hello," he said gruffly.

When she identified herself, he demanded, "Where have you been?"

She told him.

"Did you take leave of your senses?"

Laughingly, she replied, "Without doubt."

"I've been worried about you, but finally decided that your phone was out of order."

Briefly she told him of the destruction on Raccoon Creek. "I feel so sorry for those people, and I want to help them. Do you have any suggestions?"

"We can't do anything until the water goes down and the damage can be assessed. There will be plenty to do after that, I imagine. In the meantime, try to stay out of trouble. I can't imagine what Clark was thinking, to let you take such a jaunt." He hung up without giving her time to answer, so she judged that the dear doctor had more work to do than he could manage right now.

Clark didn't return from Lexington until late that afternoon, but he came with plenty of supplies. His sisters rushed out to carry in the clothes he had brought for them; since both girls were taller and heavier than Beth, they had been quite uncomfortable in her clothing all day. While Sallie and Mary Lynn happily sorted out the new garments, Clark handed Beth several bags of groceries, and a large sack of dog food, which Ranger sniffed appreciatively and then started pushing across the floor toward his feeding dish.

Clark carried a small bag from a department store when he made his last trip into the kitchen. "While I was shopping, I saw this and it reminded me of you."

Beth removed a reddish-brown sweater with gold trim from the bag. Clark pulled down a strand of her hair and laid it against the sweater fabric. The colors matched exactly.

"Thanks, Clark," she said breathlessly. She had already surmised that Clark hadn't had much coddling—

well, it had been a long time since anyone had bought her a gift, either. To realize that he hadn't wanted to bring his sisters new clothing without including something for her, gave Beth a warm, cozy feeling.

"Milton suggested that I set up temporary headquarters here at the clinic, if you have room for me to stay for a few nights," Clark informed her. "He wants me to get to the mine as soon as the roads are clear and use what equipment we have to build temporary roads for rescuing people who are trapped, or for taking them supplies. We're going to suspend mining operations until this crisis is over. The miners who haven't suffered any loss or damage will work wherever they're needed. I can make some plans over the telephone until the floodwaters run down. The little streams will recede quickly, but the Cumberland and its tributaries will be in flood for several days."

"It will be fine for you to stay here," Beth told him. "Sallie has been sleeping on the couch, and Mary Lynn on a cot in the office. You can have my bed, and I can sleep on the couch in the waiting room. It's plenty large enough for me."

"I won't take your bed!"

"Nonsense. You won't be comfortable anywhere else. You're too big for the couch—I'll take it." She put her hand on his arm. "I want you to sleep in comfort, Clark."

He bent over and kissed her hand. "You've persuaded me, and if I'm allowed, I'll take a nap while supper is being prepared. I didn't get much sleep last night."

"I hope you bought plenty of food—we've not had

much to eat. This will teach me to lay in supplies when I hear bad weather is on the way.''

Sallie and Mary Lynn both knew how to cook, so it didn't take them long to broil steaks, bake potatoes, and steam green beans. Beth tossed a salad and made iced tea while the girls prepared the rest. Beth's thoughts reverted often to Abner and Anna sleeping in the barn, without any hot food, and she imagined that their daughters were thinking of them, too. Still, the meal was a celebration that all of them were alive.

While they lingered over coffee and a serving of ice-cream cake, Beth asked Clark, ''What can I do to help those who have lost so much? That question has been plaguing me all day.''

''The federal-government agency for flood relief will be moving in as soon as the water recedes, and will set up an office in Harlan,'' Clark said. ''Funds will be available, and in some instances, the agency brings in temporary mobile homes to get the families sheltered as soon as possible. That will probably be the case here.''

''But I want to do something personally. During my devotions this morning, God led me to the verse, 'Be doers of the Word, and not hearers only.' That made me aware that I have a responsibility to help the ones who lost everything.''

Clark's eyes were warm as he looked at her. ''Then you'll think of something to do. Keep praying.''

Pam telephoned later on in the evening. ''Are you all right, Beth? I tried to contact you two days ago and didn't receive an answer. I decided the phones must be out of order."

Beth described her mountain expedition, which Pam thought was funny until she considered the dangers of such a night journey. "It gave me a whole new outlook on the ravages of floods," Beth said. "I've known about Kentucky floods for years, but we were never flooded in Warner Hollow."

"Ray's parents lost their home and everything they had a few years ago."

"The thing that hurt me most about the Randolphs' loss was all of Anna's ruined pictures. She had one wall covered with photos of her children. They're all gone and can never be replaced. It makes me feel so helpless not to be able to help them."

"It seems to me that you've done quite a lot— you're sheltering Mary Lynn and Sallie, and you walked for miles to find out if they were dead or alive."

As they continued their conversation, Beth suddenly had an idea, which she credited to divine inspiration.

"Say, Pam, do you suppose Ray and his band would be willing to do a benefit concert for the flood victims? I'd do all the publicity for it and arrange a place for their appearance."

"Ray isn't here now, but when he and the band return from Nashville, I'll ask them. They occasionally do benefit performances."

"I'd have to make some arrangements for the proceeds to be put in a trust fund, so the money could be allocated fairly."

Clark had been listening to their conversation. "I'm

sure there will be a fund set up at one of the local banks, with trustees appointed to administer it,'' he said. ''You could donate the concert proceeds to that.''

Within three days, Clark and the miners had repaired bridges between Harlan and Raccoon Creek, and when he went to bring his parents back to Harlan, Beth went with him. It was a bumpy ride in the large truck with oversize wheels, for the road had been underwater in many places, and the topsoil had washed away.

''I wonder how they've gotten along,'' Beth said as they lurched from one rut to another.

''I'm sure they're fine,'' Clark told her. He seemed to have regained the composure and confidence he'd lost on the day he'd learned that his family was trapped behind the floodwaters.

As he and Beth drove into the yard, which was still littered with mud and debris that had washed down from the hills and other properties upstream, Anna appeared in the doorway of the flooded house.

''Mother, how are you?'' Clark asked.

''Staying busy,'' she said. She motioned to the barn on the hill, where Abner stood in the entryway, his arm raised in greeting. ''We've spent most of our time up there where it's dry, but I've cleaned as much as I can. The helicopter dropped another bag, which included cleaning supplies, so I've done what I could. I've been able to get water from that spring by the barn to use for cleaning, but we had enough bottled water for drinking.''

"What about food?" Beth asked. "I brought some hot coffee and sandwiches."

"The coffee will be good, for we haven't had anything hot, but we haven't been hungry."

"I'll go up the hill and take Abner this thermos of coffee and some sandwiches," Beth offered.

"We want to take you into Harlan, Mother," Clark told her. "You can't live here until this house dries out and repairs are made."

"I know. We expected to go as soon as the road was open and take Mary Lynn and Sallie with us into Harlan. There's a stove and refrigerator in the house there, and we can sleep on the floor for the time being."

"Abner can't sleep on the floor," Beth protested. "He can take a cot from the clinic."

"Thank you." Anna glanced around their devastated home. "It could have been worse, I suppose, for we could have lost the house, too. As it is, I've been removing the wet carpet and throwing away what furniture is ruined. Strangely enough, I did find some pans and even a few dishes that are still intact."

"I need to go and see about Cheryl and the baby, Clark," Beth said. "If your sisters will be going in to Harlan with your parents, I'll invite the Carmichaels to move in with me."

"Cheryl's family lives in Pineville, and she probably will go there," Anna said. "But of course, that area is flooded, too."

After Beth took the hot coffee and sandwiches to Abner and helped him walk down the mountain, she and Clark drove up the hollow to check on the other residents. In most places mudslides had obliterated the road, so Clark followed the creek bed. He checked on all of the families, but none of the others were as poorly located as the Carmichaels, so Beth didn't think she was playing favorites in offering to take them into her home.

"After all, Cheryl is your patient," Clark assured her. "And no one else has a newborn baby."

Sam Carmichael decided that he would stay on their property for the time being, but he was pleased that Cheryl and his children would have a comfortable place to live. The truck was full with the three Randolphs, four Carmichaels, and Beth as they returned to the clinic. One of the floodgates had been opened into Harlan, so as the Carmichaels moved into Beth's home, the Randolphs moved out. Beth installed Cheryl and her family in her living room and bedroom, intending to sleep on the couch in the waiting room. Clark took a room at a motel in town.

During her busy days with the flood victims, Beth hadn't thought once about Alex, and she was surprised when he telephoned one night. They talked mostly about the flood and its aftermath.

"I'll be in Harlan County next week, so I'll telephone a day ahead and we can go out for dinner."

That night, instead of sleeping, Beth lay in a reclining position on the couch, her arms behind her head. She had to decide what to do about Alex, and that decision had to be made without regard to her feelings for Clark. What was the point of seeing Alex? He wasn't really a friend, since a friend was someone you could count on, and she'd never found him reliable that way. She already knew she couldn't fall in love with him. Even if she did, she'd learned that what Alex could give her would not guarantee her an abundant life. True, she would see the world, but she would not be able to continue her service to others. Alex wouldn't want her to practice her profession, for he had made it plain that he didn't approve of the type of work she was doing. Whether at the end of two years she stayed in Kentucky or lived elsewhere, nursing and midwifery were her calling, and she needed to be where she could pursue it—which she couldn't do junketing around Europe as Alex's wife. She left the couch, closed the door between the clinic and her apartment, so as not to disturb the Carmichaels. Then she sat at the computer and composed a note to send to his e-mail address in Lexington.

Alex,
Perhaps it would be better if we don't see one another anymore. I have enjoyed knowing you, but I have almost two years to work here in Harlan, and I don't know what I will do after that. I'm sure you'll understand.

Finally, Beth had to face the real truth—loving Clark as she did, she no longer found any enjoyment in Alex's company. On impulse, just before she sent the message, Beth sent a copy to Clark at his corporate office, as well. Though he'd never said much about Alex, she knew he worried about the other man's attentions.

* * *

The following week was busy for Beth because, as the smaller streams receded, many patients came to the clinic for treatments or shots that they'd missed during the flood. Ray Gordon had telephoned that his men would do the benefit concert, and Beth arranged to have the concert at the Harlan football field the first weekend in June during the Poke Sallet Festival when the town would be full of people. When Milton Shriver learned what she was sponsoring, he said that the mining company would match the amount of money raised at the concert.

Still not satisfied with her role in helping the flood victims, Beth came up with the idea of asking residents to donate new or used furniture to be passed on to those who had lost their homes. She arranged to have this furniture delivered to the armory during mid-May when those who had lost everything should have been provided mobile homes. After clinic hours, Beth canvased the furniture stores in the area asking for donations of slightly damaged furniture that couldn't be sold as new items. She was overwhelmed by the merchants' response, and at one large retail store in Harlan, she was told that the company would send in a trailer load of new living-room suites so that each household could have one roomful of new furniture. Beth had solicited several volunteers, including Sallie and Mary Lynn, who would work with her to see that the items were allotted equally to the fifteen families that had been affected by the flood.

The Poke Sallet Festival always generated a lot of enthusiasm throughout the entire state because it would be hard to find a Kentuckian who hadn't eaten his share of poke sallet. Pokeweed, another name for the common plant found in most states east of the Mississippi, was considered a delicacy in many rural areas. Poke shoots resembled asparagus, and the young shoots boiled in salt water and then fried in hot oil were relished, not only for the flavor, but as a spring tonic and generous source of vitamins and other minerals.

Beth had never attended the Poke Sallet Festival, but a spring season never had passed that her mother and grandmother hadn't gathered the young shoots and seen that Beth had an ample portion. The consumption of poke sallet was considered more beneficial than a trip to the doctor, and one well-known doctor was known to have said that if anyone got sick from eating poke, he would treat them without charge.

By the weekend of the festival, a degree of normalcy had returned to Harlan County, and perhaps in an effort to put the past few months behind them, the county residents, as well as visitors from throughout the state, converged on the county seat. Beth and her volunteers, including Sallie and Mary Lynn, had sold three hundred tickets for the concert, and on the evening when the concert was presented, the bleachers at the football field were filled, and some people sat on lawn chairs they had brought along. An offering was taken during intermission, and total proceeds of the evening came to more than five thousand dollars. When the coal company matched that, it would be a fund large enough to help many people.

Clark and Sam Carmichael helped at the furniture giveaway to load items for those who were eligible to receive them. Beth was surprised, when the trailer load of new furniture arrived, to be greeted by a hearty, bluff man, who rode in the passenger seat.

"Well, Miss Warner, I'm pleased to meet you. My name is Warner, too—Joel Warner."

"I've not known many people with my family name," Beth said. "I'm glad to meet you."

Mr. Warner, it turned out, was a major stockholder in the company that had donated the furniture, and he lived in Illinois.

"Since my family roots are in Harlan County, I wanted to come down and meet you. I've been tracing my family tree."

"As far as I know, I'm the only person with the Warner name around here now."

"But there used to be lots of us—back in the days when feuding was rife between the Warners and Randolphs."

Beth flashed a look at Clark, who had overheard Warner's remarks. He grinned at her and shook his head, which she took to mean that she shouldn't mention his name.

"I hope you haven't come back to stir that up! I'm friends with the only Randolphs around here."

Warner laughed heartily. "I'm too lazy to feud with anyone, but I do want to find out everything I can about the Warners who have lived here. Would you be interested in helping me? I intend to put all my findings in a book when I finish my research."

Beth didn't want to disillusion him by saying that the Warners in Harlan County couldn't bear much research, so she said, "I'll give it some thought. Why don't you leave your name and address, and I'll contact you if I decide I can contribute anything."

Later, after the furniture was unloaded and Warner had departed, Clark approached Beth.

"It's time you took a break. There are enough volunteers here that all of you should get out and enjoy the festivities part of the time. I'm taking you to the traditional poke dinner."

"You don't have to twist my arm," she replied. "I haven't had any poke greens for years. I always did like them."

So they wandered along the streets, pausing to watch the craft demonstrations—spinning, weaving, wood carving. They stood in line for an hour for their dinner, but Beth found it pleasant to chat with people she had known when she was a child, and to greet the new friends she had made at the clinic.

"This meal reminds me of home," Beth said, when they were finally seated and served the boiled poke sallet, green onions, hard-boiled eggs, crisp country bacon and fried corn cakes. Clark drank a glass of buttermilk with his meal, but Beth had never acquired a taste for buttermilk, so she ordered a glass of iced tea.

On their way back to the armory, Clark and Beth passed by the home where Beth had lived with Grandmother Blaine.

"This is where I saw you for the first time, Bethie, and I've never forgotten that impression of you. You were so pretty with your long chestnut hair flowing over your shoulders, and you wore a yellow blouse and jeans. I first noticed you when you were lifting the little boy with crutches onto the bus.''

The scene was vivid in Beth's mind, too, and she sighed. ''Lots of things have happened since then.''

''But you haven't changed. You're still helping people. For the past six weeks you haven't given one thought to yourself, and it's telling, by the way. You've lost several pounds, if I'm any judge, and there isn't much about you that I don't notice. But while I worry about your health, I do admire your compassion, Beth.''

''I couldn't have lived with myself if I hadn't done everything I could to reach out to these people. If I've been able to make a difference, then I'm content.''

Chapter Nine

Once the Poke Sallet Festival was ended, Beth considered she had done all she could do to help those who had been affected by the flood. Most of them were back on their own property now, and while some things could never be replaced, still, they were comfortable. Only time could heal their damaged emotions.

During the past few weeks Beth had fretted somewhat about her note to Alex, but when a month had passed and she hadn't heard from him, she knew he'd taken her at her word. He couldn't have cared much for her, she decided, so her conscience didn't burden her as it had when she'd turned Clark down. Clark had mentioned the message to Alex only once.

"Care to tell me why you parted company with Connor?"

"I've never discussed him with you before, so there isn't any need to start now."

"Care to tell me why you sent me a copy of the message?"

"I don't even know the answer to that myself. Let's just forget about Alex, shall we?"

With a laugh, he said, "That suits me completely."

The work at the clinic increased as the summer progressed, and Beth often felt that she was on a merry-go-round. Although, at first, the local women had been slow to accept her as a midwife, in addition to the Carmichael child, she had delivered two babies in homes, and one woman, whose small trailer wasn't equipped for a home delivery, had come to the clinic and was elated over the comfort of water birth when compared to her previous confinements. Beth was counseling two other couples for delivery at home later on in the year.

A few prenatal patients with health conditions that she considered more than she should handle, Beth had referred to Dr. Andrews; and the doctor examined all of her other maternity patients at least once, so he would be familiar with the individual cases if Beth should run into complications that required his expertise. So far, this hadn't happened. She worked overtime at her job, for she was now conducting prenatal classes for the young women.

One thing that had aided Beth both professionally and spiritually was her connection on the Internet with other nurse practitioners and midwives. These women not only believed that the natural delivery of babies provided a physical bonding between parents and child, but they considered it a spiritual experience for the family. Beth taught this concept to her patients, and she prayed often with her patients during their time of extreme labor.

She spent every Sunday with Clark, and sometimes his family, whom she invited to her apartment for dinner occasionally, for it was more convenient than the Randolphs' small house in Harlan. Quite often on Sunday afternoons, she and Clark went to Warner Hollow to check on the progress of the renovation. He had placed the marker Beth had provided at the head of her mother's grave, and now she seldom recalled the trauma of her parents' deaths. The home place no longer held any sorrow for her; she had come to terms with her childhood hang-ups.

Spiritually, her faith was stronger. She now found it easy to pray, and uplifting to read her Bible. But emotionally, she still had a long way to go. *What would she say if Clark again asked her to marry him?* Since the flood, except for the occasional spontaneous caress, Clark had not made any overtures beyond friendship; but Beth didn't doubt that he was biding his time.

One Sunday afternoon, as they were driving back from Warner Hollow, Clark said, "You need a vacation, Beth. You've lost weight, and you're looking drained."

"Nothing was said in my contract about a vacation. I assumed that I would have to work at least a year before I took holidays. Besides, where would I go?"

"I'm glad you asked." He grinned at her, and she knew he'd set her up for that question. "I'm going to take two weeks off next month, and most of that time I'll spend working at our—my house," he corrected himself quickly. "But I do intend to take a few days of vacation. Ray Gordon and I've been talking— Why can't you join the Gordons and me for a little trip around the state to some of the places you haven't seen before?"

"Still trying to sell me on Kentucky, are you?"

"Well, yes, I did have that in mind."

"You didn't have to be sneaky about it. If it will relieve your mind, I'm finding that Kentucky isn't such a bad place to live." He caught his breath and looked at her quickly, and Beth raised her hand. "Now hold on a minute. Don't jump to any conclusions. That doesn't mean I won't go somewhere else to live after I've been here two years."

"What about taking a few days off work? Whatever the reason, it will be good for you."

"If it's all right with Shriver Mining Company, I don't have any objections. I'll have to check my schedule to see when I could be away. I don't have another delivery for a couple of months. And speaking of deliveries, I must go to see Shirley. I telephone her occasionally, but I would like to see for myself how she's getting along."

"We can swing back through Lexington on our travels if you'd like to."

"But what would I do with Ranger? We certainly can't take him along. He'd take up more room in a car than I will."

"Daddy will drive out every day and look after him. It will give him something to do—he's fidgety, living in town."

"I'll have to lay in a big supply of food—I wouldn't

expect them to furnish his feed. His groceries cost more than mine do.'' With a grin, she added, ''But he's worth it.''

They arranged the trip for the following week, traveling in the Gordons' customized van, which gave plenty of room for Grace to play. It was a first for Beth to have a vacation, and since she knew that Dr. Andrews and his nurse would be capably handling her work at the clinic, she put everything out of her mind and focused on relaxation.

They went first to the Breaks Interstate Park on the Kentucky-Virginia border, where they had reservations at the lodge.

''You'll like this park, Bethie,'' Clark said, as they traveled northeastward. ''Through the ages, the Russell Fork of the Big Sandy River has carved the biggest canyon east of the Mississippi River.''

''Some people refer to it as the 'Grand Canyon of the South,''' Ray added.

Their connecting rooms at the motor lodge were luxurious, and the view out through the trees was uplifting. Ray and Clark shared one room, and Pam asked for a folding bed for Grace in the room she and Beth occupied. The food at the Rhododendron Restaurant was a treat to Beth, for with her harried schedule, she lived mostly on sandwiches and canned soups. Almost the only time she had a decent meal was when she ate with Clark's family or invited them to her apartment for dinner.

While they were eating breakfast on their first morning at the park, Pam mentioned that they must plan to go swimming. The Olympic-size pool looked inviting because the weather was hot, but Beth had never learned to swim.

"I'll sunbathe while the rest of you are in the water. I'm not prepared for swimming."

"You mean you didn't bring a swimsuit!" Pam said incredulously. "That's a must on a vacation."

"Not for me, it isn't," Beth said with a laugh. "I've never learned to swim. Remember, there wasn't much water in Warner Hollow except what we pumped from the well."

"Well, you can wear one of my suits. We're going swimming this afternoon—even Grace likes the water."

"I'll teach you to swim, Beth," Clark volunteered. "I learned to swim when I was just a boy."

"Well, I'll try it, but I'm going to look pretty awkward. I won't do as well as Grace."

"All nurses should know how to swim."

For Beth's peace of mind, the swimming was put off until afternoon, and during the morning, Clark and Beth attended a ranger's lecture and joined him on a walking tour to popular sites in the park. Grace was too young to do much hiking, so the Gordons spent the morning in more leisurely pursuits.

The ranger discussed the folklore and history of the Breaks. Of major interest to Beth was the story of John Swift, an Englishman, who had hidden a vast fortune in the area, but which no one had ever found.

They enjoyed seeing Pow Wow Cave near the State Line Overlook frequented by Shawnee Indians and later utilized by moonshiners who found the cave a great place to hide their activities from federal revenue agents. On the hike, they came across native wildlife—turkey and deer—as well as squirrels, chipmunks, and a myriad of birds.

The swimming in the afternoon wasn't as disastrous as Beth had anticipated, but the pool was so crowded that even Clark conceded it wasn't the place for swimming lessons. He did succeed in teaching her to dogpaddle a little, and Beth enjoyed the buoyancy and freedom she experienced in the water. Mostly they sunbathed on the grassy area, each of them taking turns supervising Grace in the wading pool nearby.

In the evening they drove through the park, stopping at the various overlooks. And as they slowly drove, pausing often to look out over the canyon, Beth acknowledged that Kentucky was a majestic state and that it had more to offer than she had ever imagined when she'd lived in Warner Hollow.

From the Towers Overlook they admired the imposing pyramid of rocks over half a mile long, jutting out of the forest of evergreen and deciduous trees. From this point they could observe a panoramic series of rapids and serpentine twists that offered excitement to white-water rafters during various seasons of the year.

After they left the park, they traveled westward and spent the next day at Cumberland Falls State Resort Park, where they picnicked and hiked over the trails. The abundant flow of water over the falls was an amazing sight to Beth, who had never before seen a large waterfall.

When they arrived in Lexington, the Gordons shopped at a toy store while Beth and Clark went to visit Shirley. The girl's pleasure at seeing them brought tears to Beth's eyes, but she was gratified to see that Shirley looked well.

"How are you, Shirley?"

"The nurses and doctors say I will have an easy delivery—that I'm doing just fine. Everyone is good to me. I'm doing well in my schoolwork, and am learning a lot in the prenatal classes, but I'm awful homesick, Beth."

"Why, I had no idea, Shirley! You can leave here and come home for a visit."

"Where would I visit? Mom won't allow me to come in the house."

"Maybe she's changed her mind by now."

Shirley shook her head sadly. "I don't think so. I wrote her two letters and she didn't answer, so I wouldn't write again." She smiled, with a sad little expression. "It's kind of funny. When I was living at home, I wanted to leave so badly, and I thought I would never want to see my mother again, but I do miss her—in a way, more than I do Dad."

"I see your father at the mine quite often," Clark said. "He always asks about you."

"He probably doesn't know that I've even written."

"Why don't you come and visit me for a weekend?" Beth said to her niece. "Your father could come there to see you."

But Shirley was still thinking about her mother. "Mom and I didn't get along, but I'll admit it was partly my fault. I've been pretty wild for a few years, and I'm sure it must have worried her a lot. And she hasn't had an easy time."

She looked at Clark. "You probably know, Mr. Randolph, that Dad has a girlfriend. He's never loved Mom, but when the girl he loved married someone else, he married my mother. Soon after that, his former girlfriend got a divorce, and that's when he started drinking. Mom wouldn't divorce him so he could marry the woman he wanted, but he's seen her off and on since then."

"Why, I had no idea," Beth said. "My folks never mentioned it."

"They might not have known," Clark said. "I hadn't heard about it until now."

"Dad has been cautious, but I heard plenty about it at home because Mom was always quarreling with him about *'that woman.'*"

This disclosure caused Beth to feel more compassion for Luellen.

"I've always loved Dad, for I'm sure he's been miserable being unfaithful to Mom, but he's weak. Anyway, I'd like to see them, as well as my little brothers."

"I'll take you to Harlan anytime you want," Clark offered.

"I'll think about it. And another thing, Beth. The nearer the time comes, the more I dread giving my baby away. It's a part of me, and I suppose it's because I'm separated from my family, I feel so close to the child. I know I'm not in a position to give the child a good life, but I'm going to be really sad to lose it. I've already told the supervisors here to take the baby away before I see it."

Beth's heart ached at Shirley's words. Especially

since she'd so often witnessed the unparalleled joy of a new mother bonding with her infant. Beth couldn't imagine Shirley's pain and thought the girl very strong to stick to her decision, which was, unfortunately, probably best for the baby.

After their return to Harlan County, Beth didn't see much of Clark for the next week because he was staying at his home site day and night. The carpenters had already completed the extension on the house, and the brick siding had been removed, and the old logs cleaned to bring out their natural beauty. Clark had also purchased logs from an abandoned house, which were used on the exterior of the new addition.

During his week of vacation, he'd had workers remove all of the original interior plaster and wallboard, so that he could put in insulation and install electric heat before building new walls in each room. Even the rear portion of the attic had been renovated and a bedroom and small washroom constructed there.

All that was left to do was to remove the wall between the living room and her parents' bedroom, finish the floors and open up the vaulted ceiling. Then the house would be ready for occupancy. The results were beautiful, and Beth only wished that her parents could have enjoyed the luxurious new interior that Clark had created.

Clark had indicated that he wouldn't come to Harlan at all during the week, so Beth was surprised one evening when he arrived soon after she had closed the clinic.

"Just in time for supper," she said, "if you want to risk my cooking."

"You've become a good cook, Beth. All you needed was practice. And, yes, I will eat with you, but that wasn't why I came."

He took a large envelope from his pocket. "I found this behind the fireplace mantel, when we were working on the living-room walls. I think you should have it."

The envelope was dusty and cobwebs clung to it. Beth withdrew a medal—a Distinguished Service Medal—awarded by the U.S. Army in 1944.

"Is it Daddy's?" she asked.

"There's a certificate in the envelope, too."

Her hands trembled as she read aloud, "'This Distinguished Service Medal is awarded to John Warner for meritorious service during World War II.'"

"Hadn't you seen it before?"

"It does seem vaguely familiar. I may have seen it as a child, but it has probably been behind that mantel for years."

"That's what I figured."

"Daddy talked often about his war experiences, but I didn't always pay much attention. Thank you, Clark, for bringing this to me. Mom told me that the Warners had distinguished themselves in the United States, so she probably had Daddy in mind, too. I guess I've been too critical of my heritage."

But the next day brought news that plunged Beth into the doldrums again about her family. *Why must she let her emotions swing like a pendulum where her family was concerned?*

When the evening news came on, she was stunned by the anchorwoman's opening words.

"This breaking news has just come in to our newsroom. Two former Kentucky men have been arrested in Alabama for allegedly masterminding a bogus investment scheme. Investigators estimate that the scam defrauded victims in several states of over a million dollars. The fraudulent get-rich-quick scheme attracted many elderly investors, who have since lost their life savings.

"Marvin and Clinton Warner, residents of Harlan County until last year, are the sons of the late John Warner, a recluse, who for years guarded his property in Warner Hollow with a shotgun. Authorities will be investigating the possibility that the elderly Warner was also involved.

"Our reporters will be in Harlan County tomorrow to learn what they can about the activities of the Warner brothers when they lived in this area."

Beth snapped off the set. She couldn't listen to anything else. Within ten minutes, the phone rang, and it was Clark.

"Did you hear the news?" he asked anxiously.

"Yes, to my sorrow."

"That doesn't have anything to do with you."

"You know better, Clark. Just when I've been able to let go of unhappy memories, something else happens to remind me that the Warners aren't all they should have been."

"I'm in Lexington now, but I'm coming to Harlan tomorrow evening for the weekend. How about dinner?"

"If you want to come here, that's fine. Right now, I don't know if I can ever face anyone in Harlan County again."

"Please, Bethie, don't feel that way. It isn't your fault." When she didn't reply, he said, "I'll be there by six o'clock tomorrow evening. Remember the words of the psalmist. 'But I will sing of your strength, in the morning I will sing of your love; for you are my fortress, my refuge in times of trouble.' You'll feel better in the morning."

"I hope so, Clark. I couldn't feel any worse. I'll be expecting you."

After Clark's call, Beth fastened Ranger to his leash and went past the backyard to take a favorite trail along the river. Ravages of the spring flood were still evident in the uprooted trees sprawled on the riverbed and the layers of matted brown leaves visible beneath wilting summer weeds. The leaves on the sycamores were browning, and those on the maple and beech trees had turned yellow. The sumacs gleamed brilliant red in the pale light, and flocks of birds flew from their branches when Ranger lunged at them.

Usually this trail brought peace and contentment to Beth, but not this evening. The television news about her brothers had delivered a blow to her peace of mind. Dared she admit that she had begun to think of her home in Warner Hollow with some fondness, knowing without a doubt that Clark wanted her to marry him and live there? The thought had not been displeasing to her.

But now, knowing that the whole county would be discussing her brothers' disgrace, she didn't see how she could remain here. And contemplating another year in Harlan County seemed like an eternity.

After her walk, Beth checked her e-mail. This contact with other nurse-midwives was usually a good way to end the day, for most of the messages were professionally encouraging and spiritually uplifting. She seldom posted messages herself, and most people probably forgot she was even in the loop, so she was surprised to find among the many posts a message addressed to her personally. She recognized the sender as one of the doctors she had worked with at the hospital in Pennsylvania.

Beth, I have had an inquiry from a birth center in San Diego, California, asking me to recommend one of our students for an administrator's post. This is a new facility, and it seems to be a good opportunity. I would like to recommend you. Your income would be more than adequate. Let me know soon if you are interested.

Beth downloaded the letter and looked at it long and intently. Was it a coincidence that the message came at a time when she was wrestling with a decision about leaving Harlan County for good? Or was it God's provision for her to leave her painful memories behind? Could this be the answer to her dilemma? If she was in California, she would be far away from Warner

Hollow and its unpleasant associations. She hit the re-ply-to-sender option.

I can't give you an answer right now, but I am interested enough to think and pray about it. I'll be back to you soon. Thanks for thinking of me.

If she should go to California for a job interview, she would need some new clothes, and she decided to go shopping, but she couldn't shop in Harlan tonight. Since there would be a few hours before dark, Beth drove to Pineville, hoping she wouldn't see anyone she knew. She thought it was safe enough, for Pam and Ray were her only acquaintances there, and they were away for the weekend.

Beth went into a department store in a mall that had always looked enticing. Having bought secondhand clothing for most of her life, Beth gasped more than once over the prices, but she did buy a boiled-wool cardigan in apple green, a white turtleneck blouse, and a pair of cotton pants in a miniature black-and-white check. She added a hip-stitched pleated black skirt and a matching button-front blouse in a soft microfiber polyester to her purchases. Although she was pleased with what she had bought, her hand trembled when she signed the check—she had earned this money through many hours of hard work, and it hurt to spend so much at one time.

But Clark's delight when he saw her on Saturday night wearing the new slacks and sweater made her happy that she had bought the clothes. That, however, was the only ray of happiness in the traumatic day she had endured.

She had been barraged with telephone calls from various newspapers and television and radio stations asking about her brothers. She finally stopped answering the phone, put a Closed sign on the clinic door, locked up and took refuge in her apartment with the draperies closed.

When she saw Luellen's number on the Caller ID in midafternoon, she did pick up the phone. "What are we going to do, Beth?" she cried. "These reporters are driving me crazy. I don't know anything about my brothers."

"I'm not talking to anyone," Beth told her. "And I don't like being a prisoner in my own house. Right now, I'm trying to ignore them. You'll have to do the same."

"That's easier said than done," Luellen snapped, and Beth's ear rang from the strident sound when her sister slammed down the receiver.

While she prepared the evening meal for Clark and herself, she watched on television as images of Warner Hollow were shown, and one of the clinic, and a picture of Luellen throwing a bucket of water on a reporter who came to her door. When Clark arrived, Beth was so annoyed she could hardly be civil to him.

He'd brought her a box of red roses, and she arranged them in a white vase, which she purchased in Harlan during the Poke Sallet Festival. While they ate, Clark tried to keep a conversation going, but she answered mostly in monosyllables. Eventually Clark gave up, and they ate in silence.

After they'd rinsed the dishes and put them in the dishwasher, Clark said, "Let's go for a ride, Beth. You probably haven't been out of the house all day."

"Ranger and I went for a long walk early this morning before the siege started."

"Won't you go for a ride with me?" he persisted.

She agreed, wondering why he still desired her company, when she was so cranky and lethargic. They drove for several miles in silence, until Clark made a sharp right-hand turn onto a secondary road. Beth looked at him quickly—this was the road he had taken eight years ago, the night of his senior prom. Beth hadn't been along here since that disastrous night, but every time she passed the turnoff, she thought of what had happened then.

Clark parked to one side of the road and turned off the ignition. Once the vehicle's lights were extinguished, darkness settled around them. Beth couldn't even see Clark, but she was sensitive to his presence. He moved closer to her, and his arm encircled her shoulders and pulled her gently toward him.

"Bethie..." he said and paused. Beth trembled, and he must have been aware of her reaction. How he found her lips in the darkness, Beth didn't know, for she hadn't even spoken, but his kiss was long and intense.

"Bethie," he started again.

"Please don't, Clark," she told him. "Take me back home." She knew what he intended to say, and she couldn't bear it.

"I have to talk, Beth. It's been many years since we were here before. I've come to this spot dozens of times in the past few months, thinking about us and our future. For both our sakes, we can't continue as we've been doing.''

Beth's eyes were growing accustomed to the darkness now, and she could see his face close to hers, his eyes full of emotion. She looked away, trying to concentrate on the shrill calls of the katydids echoing through the woodlands, and the plaintive hoot of an owl in the distance. Anything to forget why they were here. A gentle breeze blew through the half-open window and her long hair swirled around Clark's face.

When he started to speak again, she put her fingers over his lips, but he captured her hand in his and held it while he spoke.

''Beth, my love for you is no secret, so I don't need to tell you that. And I also think that you know that I bought the house in Warner Hollow and remodeled it for you. I want to take you there as my wife. I've waited long enough. It's been over seven years since I first knew I loved you, and I've been thinking of Jacob in the Bible who served two seven-year periods in order to take Rachel as his bride, and he said that those days 'seemed unto him but a few days, for the love he had to her.' I can wait another seven years if I have to, but I want to marry you now.''

Beth's throat constricted and her eyes moistened. She couldn't speak. Besides, what could she say when reminded of such devotion?

''I'm asking you again—I want to marry you, Bethie. God made us for each other. Can't you see that? A few months ago you thought that your lack of spiritual commitment was a detriment in our relationship.

That isn't the case anymore. You've matured in your faith. Now you're as strong spiritually as I am. As for not living in Kentucky, we can work that out someway. Will you give me the answer I want tonight?''

Beth moved out of his arms, and felt as if she were leaving the warmth of a fire for frigid temperatures. She gripped the handle of the door for support.

''Clark, I won't marry you. I'm sorry, but I just don't think I could make you happy. Not as you deserve to be. I had hoped that I had buried my hangups about the past, and I had anticipated giving you the answer you want. Then when the news began circulating about my brothers, I just gave up. It seems there's no end to the scandals that follow the Warners. Would you actually want to have me bear your children and give them such a heritage?''

''Bethie, I've tried to convince you that you aren't responsible for what your family has done. No one has lived a more exemplary life than you—I want to marry you.''

''No,'' she said coldly. It hurt to take such a harsh tone with him, but it hurt even more to keep discussing the prospect of being Clark's wife, which now seemed to Beth like a dream that would forever be out of reach. Clark made no move to touch her. The determination in her voice must have convinced him that she could not be persuaded. ''I'm going to leave Kentucky.''

She told him about the e-mail message she'd received. ''I actually believe God is presenting me with an opportunity for service in a new region. I intend to investigate the job. I'll talk to Mr. Shriver and ask him to release me from my contract, and I'll pay him back for my education. You've said that he's a reasonable man, so I believe he will grant my request, especially since he, along with the rest of the county, knows about this latest Warner escapade."

A few minutes before, Beth had tried to get Clark to stop talking and now she wished he would say something, because the silence in the vehicle was suffocating. But Clark didn't speak. He moved back under the steering wheel, started the engine, turned around in the middle of the road, and headed back toward the highway.

At the clinic, he was as solicitous as always. He opened the door, turned Ranger out of the house, looked into every room to make to make sure all was safe. Then he stood looking out the picture window until Ranger whined for admittance. When the dog was back inside, Clark went to Beth, where she sat drooped at the kitchen table. He bent down and brushed his lips across her hair.

"Goodbye, Bethie," he said, and left the building.

Usually it was "Good night," so Beth knew that Clark had taken her words as final. He was finished with her, and she couldn't blame him.

The next day seemed long without Clark, for they had spent every Sunday together for months. Beth didn't go to church; she didn't want to encounter Clark or his family. She doubted that they would want to see her, either. It was a miserable day except for the fact that the reporters had finally stopped pestering her.

Once, Beth started to send an e-mail message that she was interested in going to California for an interview at the birth center, but even as she had the cursor on the new-message icon, something stayed her hand. *Wait another day.* So, not knowing why, she waited.

Beth was always busy on Monday mornings, and the time passed more quickly than she thought it would. She doubted that anyone would come to the clinic, but she had to be ready, and to her surprise, a few patients came. She answered the phone in late morning to Dr. Andrews's harried voice.

"Have you heard about the trouble at Shriver Mine No. 10?"

"No."

"There's been an explosion, and several men are trapped. We'll need all the medical assistance we can get. Close the clinic and come as soon as possible."

When Beth announced this news to the two patients in the waiting room, they left hurriedly without a word. Shriver No. 10 was the mine where all the locals worked, so if a tragedy had occurred, almost everyone in the county could be affected.

Quickly Beth gathered all of the supplies she thought might be helpful, and as she drove through Harlan and headed up the hollow where the mine was located, she thought of her childhood days when disasters had killed dozens of men. She recalled going to one funeral where four caskets were lined up in front of the church. All were members of one family—a father and his three sons. She had never forgotten the stricken look on the face of that widow and mother.

"But mines are safer nowadays," she argued aloud

with herself. "There won't be anything like that now."

Automobile travel had slowed to a crawl along the narrow road, and more than once, she had to pull off to the side to allow emergency vehicles to pass. A panel truck from a TV station in Lexington followed in the wake of the ambulances. Beth turned on her caution lights and pulled out ahead of the other traffic. A half mile short of the mine, she was stopped by a security guard.

"Sorry, ma'am, no one but miners' families are allowed in."

"I'm a nurse, and Dr. Andrews sent for me."

"In that case, go on through. We're just trying to stop the curiosity seekers."

She wanted to ask him the extent of the crisis, but he turned away to stop another car. When she neared the mine, she was waved into a field to park. Grabbing her bag of supplies, Beth ran along the road. She saw Dr. Andrews's car and, to her surprise, Clark's vehicle, but she should have known he would be here—it was part of his job to check out emergencies.

Four patients were lying on blankets not far from the mine's entrance. Dr. Andrews was working with the emergency-vehicle drivers to prepare the injured men for the drive to the hospital. He nodded at Beth.

"These four were near the entrance when the explosion occurred, and they were able to escape. Some of them have broken bones, so just assist me. I'm giving them a quick examination before we send them to the hospital."

Beth slipped on a pair of latex gloves and passed

the required instruments to the doctor as he knelt by each miner in turn. At least two of the men had broken legs, and all of them had abrasions.

"How many more inside?" Beth whispered.

"As many as ten, probably. The morning shift had just started, and all the miners weren't in yet."

As she helped the doctor, the area filled with people, and Beth's compassion went out to them—their grim, pale faces indicated their inner feelings. The thing that stunned her, however, was the hush that enveloped the mine yard. In spite of the throng of worried people, the emergency vehicles moving in and out, and the mining equipment being readied for use, silence hovered over the area. She scanned the crowd for Clark, but she didn't see him.

When Dr. Andrews had made the injured as comfortable as possible, the four men were dispatched by ambulance to the hospital in Harlan. The doctor sat down wearily on a bench. "After all these years, you'd think I would be expecting these disasters, but every time, I'm shocked and surprised. I always believe it can't happen again."

"What caused this blast?"

"I don't know. The odor of gas had been reported on Friday, and that's the reason Clark came here to investigate this morning."

Startled, Beth turned to look at Dr. Andrews. "Clark? Where is he?"

Without meeting her gaze, he jerked his hand toward the mine's entrance. "He was the first one to go in this morning. He wanted to be sure it was safe for the others. Apparently, it wasn't." He reached out and took Beth's hand. "I'm sorry I'm the one who had to tell you."

Chapter Ten

Beth had never felt such a sense of desolation and shock. Her head spun. She wound her arms around her waist and would have fallen over if Dr. Andrews hadn't supported her. Not even the day she had lost both of her parents had she felt as helpless and alone as she did now. She saw Abner and Anna Randolph and their daughters approaching, and she ran to them.

"I just heard," she whispered.

"Now don't fret, Beth," Abner said. Though she saw the anxiety in his eyes, he patted her on the shoulder as if she were a child. "Hold on to your faith."

Beth turned and looked at Clark's mother, and the peace and serenity usually displayed on her face was gone. Her expression was stolid; there was a resignation in her eyes. Was Anna remembering that other time when her husband was imprisoned underground, only to live and be handicapped for the rest of his life? Thinking of Clark's sturdy, lean body and his quick, easy steps, Beth couldn't bear the thought that even if

Clark lived, he might have to go through life disabled as his father was.

Perhaps reading her thoughts, Abner said, "There are many kinds of disability, Beth, and no matter what happens to Clark, his spirit will never be crippled."

A sob escaped her lips though she was dry-eyed, and she threw her arms around Clark's mother. Anna's composure slipped a little, for Beth felt her tremble.

"I love him, Mrs. Randolph, and I've never told him. Just two nights ago, he asked me again to marry him, and I refused. What if I never have another chance?"

Anna shook Beth roughly and looked deep into her eyes. "Get control of yourself, Beth. You're Kentucky born and bred. For centuries, Kentucky women have given their men to this land. It's part of our heritage. My heart is weeping, too, but I refuse to mourn until I know I have something to mourn for. With God, all things are possible. You're a nurse—forget your own sorrow and see what you can do for these others who are fearful."

Beth swallowed hard. "You're right, of course, but I just now learned that Clark was inside the mine, and it devastated me."

Anna patted her on the back. Their attention was diverted by a Shriver Mining Company van that sped into the area. Several company officials stepped out and one of them was Milton Shriver. His face paled as he surveyed the activity around them—rescue teams moving into the mine shaft, equipment poised ready to remove the rubble when it was deemed safe enough, and the crowds of men, women, and children standing in disconsolate groups…waiting.

Milton approached his sister, and Beth moved away. She took aspirin out of her bag, picked up a jug of water and paper cups from the canteen that the Red Cross had already set up, and moved from family to family to see if she could be of any help.

Beth greeted people who had lived in her neighborhood when she was a girl and whom she hadn't seen for years. One man, Cecil Tanner, shook hands with her warmly. His wife had abandoned him years ago, and he had reared five children alone.

"How are your children, Mr. Tanner?"

Pointing toward the mine, he said grimly, "My youngest is inside, there." But his face brightened, and he said, "They're all doing well, Beth. Two of my girls are teaching school. All my kids have made me proud."

So Mr. Tanner and his children hadn't run away from a family scandal. They had stayed on and triumphed in spite of the gossip and the story that would always follow them.

She saw many other people to whom life had brought one distress after another. One man's son was serving a life imprisonment.

Stella Harvey had lost her home in order to pay the debts her son had incurred, but she was here today— waiting to hear news of that same son who was trapped inside the mine.

And when Beth stopped before one woman, she recognized her as Melissa Brownlee, the woman who had lost her husband and three sons in another mine disaster. Melissa had overcome that sorrow, and today waited with her daughter—anxious over the fate of a grandson.

As Beth circulated among the crowd, Abner, leaning heavily on his cane, followed her, offering prayer and comfort through the Scriptures. While he encouraged them to hope that their loved ones were safe, he urged them to cling to the assurance that there was a better life to come.

To keep from thinking about the possibility that Clark wouldn't survive this accident, Beth repeated over and over one verse that she'd heard Abner quote: "'Have mercy on me, O Lord, for I am in trouble.'"

In his ministry to the people, Abner often referred to the story of Job, a man who had lost everything but his life. Job's words in the face of adversity were encouraging: "'But He knoweth the way I take: when He hath tried me, I shall come forth as gold.'" And there was another verse that Beth didn't know how Abner could bear to quote: "'The Lord gave, and the Lord hath taken away; blessed be the name of the Lord.'"

Beth was heartily ashamed of herself. All her life she had run from personal problems—had acted as if she was the only one who had lost parents, or been poor, or who had scandalous relatives. She had been embarrassed because of her brothers, who had been in trouble for as long as she could remember. Could she have improved their lives if she had been more tolerant toward them? Beth wished that she could relive the past, but she knew that was impossible. *What would she do with her future?*

Near the mine shaft she came face-to-face with her sister, Luellen, who stood with her arms around her two sons.

"Luellen! Is Joe inside?"

Luellen nodded. "He went in right behind Clark Randolph, they say."

"Oh, Luellen, I'm sorry." Beth moved closer and hugged her, not stopping to wonder if she would be rebuffed. Strangely enough, Luellen returned the embrace, and tears glistened in her eyes when Beth released her.

"I always feared this would happen to Daddy," she said. "But he escaped. Somehow, I never thought it would be Joe."

Beth hugged her again and moved on, looking toward the mine opening, hoping for news. For some reason, they couldn't establish any radio contact with the men trapped inside. Although Clark seldom went anywhere without his cell phone, he'd left it in his vehicle, so they couldn't contact him that way.

Since the majority of the people here were members of Abner's congregation, he encouraged them to come together rather than stay in isolated groups.

"Let us worship," he said. "And we can do that better when we are in close communion. Let's sing praises to God."

Beth moved with the others until they formed a tight-knit group in front of Abner, who sat down on a loading platform. Under his leadership, they sang, but the words stuck in Beth's throat. *How could they sing?*

Those faces, upturned to Abner, craved words of comfort, and when he started to speak, a hush fell over the group. Beth was aware of the activity behind them as rescue teams worked in perfect order. In the distance, she heard a church bell ringing in Harlan. A cardinal perched on an electric pole and sang.

"I've been asked the question often this morning—'Why does God let terrible things like this happen?'—and dare I confess, I may have wondered, too, for my boy is trapped inside. I wish I had an answer to that question, but I don't. I've never been able to put an answer to 'Why do good people have to suffer?'"

He tried to open his Bible with one hand, but the wind was riffling the pages, and Mary Lynn went to stand beside her father, and spread the Bible open at his direction.

"But I do know this," Abner continued. "We are people of faith. We can't explain why the sun rises and sets as it does. We don't know why the seasons come and go as they do. We simply accept, by faith, that these natural occurrences will be timely. Let me repeat—we are people of faith, and when we start questioning God, that means we no longer trust Him, that we no longer have faith."

He turned to Mary Lynn. "Read from the Book of Daniel, chapter three, verses seventeen and eighteen."

"Daddy, I can't read now," she pleaded.

"Daughter, you're a person of faith. Read the verses."

In a faltering voice that gained strength as she continued, Mary Lynn read, "'If we are thrown into the blazing furnace, the God we serve is able to save us from it, and He will rescue us from your hand, O king. But even if he does not, we want you to know, O king,

that we will not serve your gods or worship the image
of gold you have set up.'''

Abner nodded his thanks to Mary Lynn and she
stepped off the platform and joined her mother.

"You're familiar with this biblical story. The three
Hebrew children refused to worship idols, and the king
threatened punishment in the fiery furnace. The most
important message in that whole story is found in two
words—*even if*. My friends, that's faith. The three men
knew that God had the power to protect them, but they
said, '*Even if He does not,* we will still serve Him.'''

Abner continued to hold the attention of the crowd,
although occasionally someone would cast a quick
look toward the mine entrance.

"What all of us must acknowledge today is that we
believe that God has the power to work miracles and
bring our loved ones out of that mine unharmed."
Here his voice intensified in volume and passion. "But
even if He does not, our faith in Him will not falter,
and we will leave this place, saying, 'The Lord gave,
and He hath taken away; blessed be the name of the
Lord.'''

The short service did have a calming effect on those
who had listened, for when Beth and the canteen
workers moved among the people again, they accepted
sandwiches and beverages, and many welcomed the
medications she offered.

Late in the afternoon Shirley Rupe came to the mine
site, having been brought by a counselor at the residence in Lexington. Shirley looked large and cumber-
some in her advanced pregnancy. Clumsily, she ran

toward her mother, but when Luellen saw her coming, she turned her back.

"Mother," Shirley pleaded, but Luellen ignored her.

Shirley lowered her head and seemed on the verge of collapse, but the woman with her led her away. Beth went immediately to the sorrowing girl.

"Come, Shirley, stay beside me. Your mother isn't herself right now."

"Oh, she's herself, all right," Shirley muttered.

Beth had met the counselor when she had been in Lexington, and she shook hands with her. "It was good of you to bring her."

"Has there been any news?"

"Nothing at all. Rescue teams are moving into the mine as quickly as they can, but the men are apparently quite a distance into the tunnel."

"Since her mother won't accept Shirley, can you look after her until the men are found?" the woman asked.

"Of course," Beth replied. "I intend to stay here. Shirley can rest in my car if she needs to. How is she getting along physically?"

"Her due date is two weeks away, but the baby can come at any time. She shouldn't be down here, but she was so distressed when she heard about her father that we decided staying in Lexington would probably be harder on her than coming to see about him. You'll need to watch her closely."

It was nine o'clock in the evening when the news circulated that some of the men had been reached, and very soon emergency workers rushed from the shaft carrying two stretchers.

"Rupe and Randolph." The word spread quickly. Pulling Shirley with her, Beth hurried over to the rescuers, but she made way for Clark's parents. The urge to rush to him, to look into his eyes and shower him with kisses of relief and love was so great, she bit down painfully on her lip as she held herself back. After all, she had no right to be at his side. With painful regret, she put her arm around Shirley and went to check on Joe Rupe.

"I'm all right, Daddy," Beth heard Clark say, and she murmured a quick, "Thank You, God."

"Are you sure you're not hurt bad?" Anna asked.

"I've got a lot of bruises, but Joe was thrown a long way from the force of the blast. Take care of him."

"Rupe is dead," Beth heard Dr. Andrews say, and Luellen let out a squall that echoed around the hollow.

"Oh, Dad!" Shirley cried, and pulled away from Beth and ran to the stretcher. She quickly removed the blanket that covered her father, and smoothed back his hair. In spite of the scratches on his face, and the dirt-encrusted hair and beard, Joe looked more peaceful than Beth had ever seen him. Luellen moved to the cot and pushed Shirley aside. The girl stumbled and fell against Beth. Shirley grabbed her stomach and groaned, and Beth put both arms around her to support her trembling body.

After making a cursory examination of Clark, Dr. Andrews came quickly to Beth's assistance. He understood the situation at once.

"Clark is all right," he said, "but we'll take him to the hospital for tests." He checked Shirley's pulse and ran his hand over her heaving stomach.

"You've got problems here. Can you handle her at the clinic or do you want to bring her to the hospital?"

"You'll probably have all you can do at the hospital," Beth replied, waving toward the mine.

"I imagine so. According to Clark and the rescue team, the others are badly injured, although Joe is the only fatality so far. They'll have them out of the mine in another hour."

"I'll take Shirley to the clinic," Beth said. "If I run into trouble, I'll bring her to the hospital, but when I visited her in Lexington a couple of weeks ago, the nurse there said she was doing well. This may be false labor brought on by the shock. She may not deliver tonight."

"Let me know if you need help," Dr. Andrews said, and called to a man standing nearby to help Beth take Shirley to her car. Shirley was doubled up with pain, but except for a muted moan that occasionally escaped her lips, she endured her misery in silence. *Another example of a hardy Kentucky woman,* Beth thought. As she considered what she had witnessed throughout this day—the patient endurance of the women who had steeled themselves for a calamity, but yet had waited in hope—her pride in being a Kentuckian was so great that it amazed her.

"Do you need any help taking her farther?" the man asked when they reached Beth's car, and he assisted Shirley into the front seat.

"I don't think so. Shirley, you'll be able to walk into the clinic, won't you?"

Shirley grabbed the dashboard as another pain hit her, and she doubled over, but she nodded her head, so Beth thanked the man and put the car into motion.

After they had traveled about a mile, Shirley breathed deeply. "Is it going to be any worse than this?" she asked.

Beth laughed lightly. "I'm afraid so, but you'll be all right."

"Are you going to take care of me?"

"I can manage quite well at the clinic, but if you prefer to go to the hospital, Dr. Andrews will deliver your baby. This birth will be different than what you've been told to expect at a hospital, but I've assisted at the delivery of several babies since I've been here, and all has gone well."

"Although I like Dr. Andrews, I'd rather have you with me," Shirley said. "You're about the only friend that I have. I suppose you saw how Mom turned her back on me."

"Your mother was under a lot of stress tonight. You'll have to forgive her. She has lost a husband."

"And she's always loved him, even if he didn't love her."

"That couldn't have been an easy life, Shirley."

"I suppose not, but I do wish she'd welcomed me. At least, I'm glad you're family. I'm scared, and I feel mighty alone."

"You're not alone, Shirley. I'll take care of you and your baby," Beth assured her niece as she patted her hand.

At the clinic, Beth helped Shirley remove her clothes, and before she put on a voluminous gown, Beth monitored the fetal heart rate with a fetoscope. All seemed well.

"Let me get some food for you to eat while I make some preparations."

"Won't food make me sick?"

"A light snack will be good for you. You must eat—this is going to be a long night. I'll make a slice of toast and some tea."

Ranger padded around the kitchen quietly, looking from Beth to Shirley as if he knew something was amiss. He put his head on Shirley's knee, and she petted him.

While Shirley ate, Beth filled the bathtub with warm water. She had decided to use the birthing stool, rather than attempt a water birth, but the early labor pains would be less severe if Shirley could relax occasionally in the warm water.

For the next few hours, Beth walked with Shirley until the pains became unbearable, then she helped her into the warm water, sat beside her and rubbed her back and shoulders. She checked the temperature of the water frequently, draining water and adding more to keep it at a warm, comfortable temperature.

Believing that the birth of the child, in spite of the circumstances of its conception, should be a spiritual experience, Beth prayed with Shirley and read passages from the Psalms.

When the suffering was most severe, Shirley cried. "Mom!" not even realizing what she'd said. When her patient grew weary of the water, Beth helped her to walk, for she wanted to keep her on her feet as much as possible. After several hours, while they were in the kitchen and Beth was preparing a small milk shake for Shirley to sip, the doorbell rang, and the sound startled them both. Beth glanced at the clock over the kitchen sink—four in the morning.

Shirley's face brightened a little, and Beth figured she thought that Luellen had come.

Ranger, who had taken every step with them when they'd walked, was resting in his bed, but with a yelp, he headed toward the door, his tail wagging in delight, so Beth knew the caller was someone the dog knew.

"Beth, open the door." Recognizing Clark's voice, Beth was faint with relief as she struggled with the lock. As soon as she switched on the light and unlocked the screen door, Clark stepped inside, grabbing her in a bear hug. But he quickly released her. Beth was laughing and crying at the same time. She threw her arms around Clark, and he winced.

"Careful," he warned. "I have several cracked ribs."

"Oh, Clark, what if I'd never seen you again!"

"Don't dwell on what might have been. The Lord was gracious to spare me when He took others, so He must still have a purpose for me in life."

"Was there anyone else besides Joe?"

"One other man is critical, and Dr. Andrews says that he probably won't survive."

Clark looked over Beth's shoulder and saw Shirley at the table. "Dr. Andrews told me about Shirley, so I came out as soon as he released me. How are things going?"

"Slow," Shirley replied.

"She's doing fine, but it often takes longer with a first child. Probably a few more hours."

"What can I do?" Clark asked.

"Don't you need to rest? You've been through a terrible experience today."

"But not as bad as the rest of you, who didn't know what had happened to us. I'm not leaving you, so you might as well tell me what to do."

"Then you can walk with her," Beth said. "Ranger and I have been doing it for hours, and we're about bushed."

Clark laughed as he looked at the dog, lying flat on his stomach, his four legs stuck out from his body. "Well, I'm glad you've had some help. I told you that Ranger was a valuable addition to this clinic. Come on, Shirley, let's go." Gently, he took Shirley's arm and led her from the room and into the clinic. Beth closed the door behind them.

Breathing a prayer for courage, Beth dialed Luellen's number. Her sister answered immediately. Beth had been sure that she wouldn't be asleep.

"Luellen, this is Beth. Shirley is here at the clinic, and she'll be having her baby in a few hours. She's doing fine, but you know what labor pains are like, and she's scared. She needs her mother."

"She should have thought of that before she left home."

Beth could have reminded Luellen that the girl had been driven from her home, but she didn't.

"In light of all that's happened, don't you think it's time to let bygones be bygones and come to your daughter? She's facing a worse crisis than the labor pains—she's agreed to give her baby up for adoption because she has no means to care for it, and in the hospital at Lexington, she wouldn't have seen the child. But here it's different, and once she sees that baby, to lose it will be her second loss today."

Luellen's heavy breathing sounded in Beth's ear. "I beg you, Luellen, come and be with your daughter—don't miss seeing the birth of your first grandchild. I know you're in pain now, but can't you see how losing Joe so unexpectedly should make us put aside anger and pride and cherish the family we have? Luellen, in so many ways Shirley is still just a child herself."

Luellen's answer was unintelligible and with a choked sob, she hung up the phone.

When she considered it was time for Shirley to sit on the birthing stool, Beth told Clark she could handle everything from then on, and he could go to the living room and rest. As she knelt beside Shirley, the door opened behind Beth, and she looked over her shoulder. Luellen was poised on the threshold.

Shirley smiled weakly, and she relaxed under Beth's hands. "Please stand behind her and support her shoulders," Beth said matter-of-factly, as if there hadn't been any question that Luellen was expected. Luellen hesitated for only a moment before she moved to Shirley, and bent to kiss the girl on the forehead. In spite of her pain, Shirley smiled contentedly.

"Just be brave, daughter. I've been through this three times, and it's worth all of the pain after you see your own child."

"But I can't keep it, Mom. I'm arranging an adoption through the residence."

"We'll talk about that later," her mother said. "Push, Shirley."

Within a half hour, Shirley had delivered a healthy, squalling boy, and tears rolled down the new mother's face when Beth handed the baby to her.

"I want to call him Joe—Joe Rupe," Shirley said, and Luellen laid her hand on the boy's head.

"We'll take him home as soon as you feel like traveling."

"Oh, Mom, may I really keep him?"

Grimly, Luellen replied, "I've lost one Joe Rupe today, but God has given us another. 'The Lord gave, and the Lord hath taken away.' I'll help you take care of him, and God willing, I hope to be a better grandmother than I've been a mother."

"I'm sorry I caused you so much trouble, Mom."

"Both of us have a lot of forgiving to do, but you rest now. Is there a bed where we can put them, Beth? I'll stay with her while you get some sleep."

After Shirley was resting comfortably on the clinic's hospital bed with baby Joe nursing contentedly, Beth entered her apartment wearily. Clark had kicked off his shoes and had collapsed across her bed. He lay on his back, snoring gently. A large blue knot was visible below his hairline, and there were several abrasions on his hands and arms. When she leaned over and kissed him on the forehead, he mumbled in his sleep, then turned over onto his left side.

Beth got two blankets from the closet. She spread

one gently over Clark's weary body, and wrapped the other one around herself and lay down on the couch.

Sunlight was gleaming in the window when Beth awakened to the aroma of coffee. She got up and peered into the kitchen. Clark sat at the table, but he'd heard her stirring, and, walking stiffly, he came to her.

"What time is it?"

"Ten o'clock. Want some coffee?"

"Yes, but I should check on my patients."

"Everything is all right in there. I've already served them coffee and toast. Luellen is planning to take Shirley *and* the baby home as soon as you release her. I'll drive them back. Mr. Shriver wants me to help her with funeral arrangements at the company's expense."

"I feel terrible about Joe. But some good news came from the tragedy," Beth said with a sigh. "Luellen and I have made some peace with each other. It's hard to be estranged from your family, and she and her children are all I have."

"It seems as if Luellen accepts Joe's death easier than if she had lost him to divorce."

"I feel sorry for her."

Clark ruffled her hair. "You always feel sorry for people. Now feel sorry for me, and eat the breakfast I made for you. Luellen was napping when I peeked in a few minutes ago, so they don't need you now."

"I don't want anything to eat right now, but I will take a cup of coffee, if you're serving," she added with a grin.

"With pleasure."

When Clark brought the coffee, he sat down beside

her on the couch. Beth knew the next move in their relationship was up to her, for she believed that Clark would never again ask her to marry him. She reached for his hand, and his strong, tapered fingers quickly closed around hers.

"I had a lot of time to think yesterday," she began, "and some of the things I thought were so important to me, seemed very insignificant when I was faced with a major tragedy."

"I did a lot of thinking, too. Most of the time I was convinced that we would be rescued, but there were moments of doubt. What did you think about, Bethie?"

"I thought about the old adage, 'The third time is the charm,' and I decided that if a certain man asked me to marry him a third time that my answer would be a resounding 'Yes.'"

His fingers squeezed hers. "And who is this lucky man?" he asked lightly.

"You should know." She grinned. "In fact, you're the only man who has ever asked me. Maybe I shouldn't tell you that, or you'll think no one else would have me."

"Not likely. You're serious about this?" The slight trembling note in his otherwise-husky voice made her heart ache with love. She couldn't answer—only nodded. Clark immediately moved closer and enveloped her in a hug that stole her breath away. For a moment, he buried his face in her shoulder, then his lips met hers in a long, deep kiss. When he finally moved away and smiled down at her, she thought his warm brown eyes glistened with unshed tears—tears of joy.

"Where do you intend for us to live?" he asked with a speculative gleam in his eyes.

"In Harlan County. If anyone is ever going to live down the blot on the Warner name, it's up to me."

He gave her a quizzical smile. "What made you change your mind?"

"Lots of things. First, when I thought you might be lost to me, I realized that I couldn't be happy anywhere without you. Wherever you are—that's home. Then, too, I made a spectacle of myself when I first learned you were in that mine. Your mother gave me a good shaking and told me to act like a Kentucky woman ought to."

Clark laughed. "She's shaken me a few times, too, and I wouldn't put it past her to do it again if I get out of line."

"Then I decided I had to accept my family for what they are and not let their actions ruin my life. Mom told me years ago that I could be proud of my Warner ancestors. I've decided I'm going to accept Joel Warner's invitation to search out my genealogical roots, so when my children come along, I'll have it all down in black and white to prove that they have a glorious heritage."

"Any family tree will have a few 'bad apples' on it. The Warners aren't any exception."

"I'm ashamed it's taken me so long to realize that, but probably the most revealing incident of yesterday was that I learned very well what Kentucky women are like when I walked among those families who feared that they had lost the ones dearest to them. They were afraid, but they still had a hopeful look in their eyes. As your mother said, they wouldn't grieve until they knew they had something to grieve for. In the midst of their worries, they retained their belief that God was still in control. I may have to learn a lot more before I can be that trustful, but it's something I hope to achieve in time. In fact, I'll dread having you go back into another coal mine, but perhaps I'll learn to live with it.''

"Do you want to know what decision I came to while I waited to be rescued?" He pulled her into a close embrace again and winced. "I'll squeeze you, but don't you touch me. My ribs are sore. But back to yesterday... I decided that I wasn't ever going to be separated from you again, and if you moved to California, I was going with you. For although you've never told me, I was sure you do love me."

"Yes, Clark, I've loved you since the first time we met, but I was too stubborn to listen to my heart."

"Then you will marry me, Bethie? Don't you agree that God made us for each other?"

"Yes, I do. I believe that God had a plan for my life, and that plan is fulfilled in you. I want to marry you."

"'Jacob served seven years for Rachel; and they seemed unto him but a few days, for the love he had to her,'" Clark quoted, with a smile hovering around his lips, and then he kissed Beth and kissed her and kissed her until the sound of a baby's crying in the next room brought them back to reality.

* * * * * *

Dear Reader,

I've received many questions from readers about my writing style, and one in particular that may interest you is, "Do pieces of your own life experiences creep into your stories?"

My books are not autobiographical to the extent that I've written about my personal romances or family affairs. My writing reflects the national and international trips that we've taken—in fact, some of our traveling has been planned to research a particular book I was writing. Furthermore, my outlook on life and my values stem from the childhood training I received at our small Baptist church, of which I'm still an active member.

But most of all, my work mirrors my Scotch-Irish familial heritage and the influence of my childhood in a rural setting on my parents' farm. I'm a native of West Virginia, where I've lived all of my life. Both my father and my mother were born in this same community. Four of my books have West Virginia settings. In this book I've moved a few miles westward and placed my characters in eastern Kentucky, a section much like our West Virginia mountains, for the same conditions and situations existed in the development of both states.

The psalmist wrote, "I lift up my eyes to the hills—where does my help come from? My help comes from the Lord, the Maker of heaven and earth." (Psalm 121:1-2) Because of the ever-present witness of God through His creation, rural people learn at an early age to depend upon the God of the universe. I'm grateful to my ancestors for many things, but especially for settling, in the early nineteenth century, in the rural area where we live.

I would be happy to hear from you at: P.O. Box 2770, Southside, West Virginia 25187.

Irene B. Brand